"I don't understand. This doesn't make any sense. If I'm dead, why don't I remember dying?" Her hands are balled into fists so tight that the outline of her collarbone is visible through her sweater. She slams a fist against the wall, and I flinch even though the blow makes no sound. "I don't want to be dead!"

"I'm sorry. I don't understand either." *I* remember dying. I remember the horrible things he did to me, the pain, the fear, the anger, the hatred, the hope … And then the absence of everything, both welcome and terrible. I remember everything. With perfect clarity.

P With Perfect Clarity

JAMIE FERGUSON

BLACKBIRD PUBLISHING

With Perfect Clarity

Published by Blackbird Publishing, LLC
www.blackbirdpublishing.com

Cover design: Andrew Brozyna, www.ajbdesign.com
Cover images: Shutterstock, PunchStock, Library of Congress
Interior design: Blackbird Publishing, LLC

Library of Congress Control Number: 2013906036

ISBN-10: 1939949009
ISBN-13: 978-1-939949-00-4

Printed in the United States of America.

For Harry and Lulu.

With Perfect Clarity

JAMIE FERGUSON

One

Being dead is like watching an endless movie — forever observing, but never participating. Sometimes it makes me want to scream — sometimes I do scream. It doesn't matter whether I do or not. No one can hear me anyway.

There's a real movie — a ghost story — playing on the television set at the front of the store. I've seen it a thousand times. The ghost moves furniture, makes noises, and eventually manages to communicate with the living. But it's just a movie — none of those things actually work. I've tried, over and over and over.

I wrinkle my nose at the screen as I walk by.

My footsteps slow as I pass the end of the row of Action and Adventure DVDs, trailing my fingertips along the wall as I trace the boundaries of my home, my prison, my world. I reach the window and pause, looking out through where my reflection should be, and watch the rain patter on the pavement in front of the store. I miss the chill of raindrops flung against my face by the autumn winds, their refreshing coolness in the sweltering heat of the summer. I wrap my arms around myself, squeezing so tight it hurts. I *feel* real, but if I were outside the rain would fall right through me.

It's been a dreary November day — the rain steady, the kind you can walk through quickly without a coat, but if you stay outside too long you'll be soaked to the skin. It's been raining like this since early morning, around three o'clock, or maybe four? Now it's late afternoon; the sky is almost black, and the streetlights thrust harsh, bright beams through the gloom, everything that's not illuminated made darker in comparison.

A couple passing by stops underneath the oak tree in front of my window, the branches that shaded the store in the summertime now naked and forlorn without their leaves. They're arguing about something and are both quite animated. The man makes sweeping gestures with his hands, and the woman crosses her arms and taps her right foot. Her high-heeled shoes are pink and have very pointy toes. Very wet pointy toes, now, as she's standing in a small puddle. I press my nose flat against the glass and wonder what they're saying. The woman spins around, little streams of water spraying out from the ends of her hair, and marches down the street. Her companion grimaces, then rushes after her.

I step back from the window, my voyeurism unsatisfied by the brief drama, and start walking along the east wall, then jump to the side as a teenage girl plows around the corner in front of me. Her chestnut hair is glossy in the fluorescent light, and her pale face is blank, almost solemn. Her blouse is made from a bright, flowery fabric that seems far too happy for her to wear, and her jeans are a few shades darker than my own. She stomps past me, her footsteps firm. Her eyes slide over me, unseeing. I turn my head and watch her march on by, then I continue on, my own feet soundless as always.

I make my way over to the dark red sofa and plop down, the tangibility of the cushions inflexible against my nonexistent body. If I chose to I could slide right through the sofa instead of rest on top of it. Yet another inexplicable conundrum of being a ghost, like when I feel my heart thump away when I see Matt, even though my physical heart is long gone, rotted in the ground somewhere with the rest of my body. It bothers me to move through things even though I know I'm not real, not in the manner that I used to be, at least. There's something disturbing about seeing yourself *inside* something else, even if it makes sense. As much sense as possible, that is. I place my feet on the cushion and stare up at the ceiling, remembering how fresh and bright it looked the last time it was painted. Now, in 2003, it's worn, tired, the paint dirty and peeling a bit in the corners, just like the rest of the building. Just like me.

I've been trapped here for more than a century, unable to leave, unsure if I'll ever be able to. Things have changed, of course. The original house — *his* house — is gone, burned to the ground twenty-two years after I died. This house, which has since been converted into a video store, was built a few years later on the same spot, but slightly off center. Apparently I am constrained by the boundaries of the house in which I died, but the new house doesn't exactly match those boundaries, so I can go a few feet outside the store to the north, but can't reach the west wall inside.

I remember old stories that told about ghosts needing to accomplish some task before they could move on, so I've always supposed I must have something to do, but I can't seem to determine what it is. I can't do much in my ethereal state anyway, but I've tried everything I can think of, hoping year after year that I'll figure out whatever it is, hoping that there really is something to be figured out. I've attempted to talk to the living, but of course they never hear me. I've tried to leave — to escape — but the walls of the old Colorado farmhouse, of my prison, have remained steadfast even though the physical walls turned to ashes long ago. I've scoured my memory, going over and over every single thing I can recall from my nineteen years of life, but I haven't been able to come up with anything I did or didn't do that would have caused me to be bound here. Revenge or justice seem plausible in the movies, but how can I get revenge or justice when my murderer must be dead himself by now? I can't tell anyone anything. I can't leave this place. And I can't even do half the things ghosts in movies can. So how could I possibly avenge myself?

I squirm around and sit upright, my feet dangling just above the floor. I tug on the hem of my T-shirt so the fabric lies straight. Revenge wouldn't bring me back to life anyway, so what good would it be? All I want is to move on, to go wherever everyone else goes when they die. I kick my sneakered feet against the sofa, my blows as ineffectual as ever. I sigh and rest my elbow on the arm, propping my head up with my fist. I won't give up. Someday I'll figure out what I'm supposed to do. Someday.

Several customers walk by; a short, stout man and his three boys, two of whom are arguing over which movie to rent. I ignore them all, wallowing in my melancholy. The third child ignores them too. He's playing a portable video game and is completely absorbed. He stops in front of the couch, then sits down on top of me, *in* me. For a split second I *am* him —

… I kick ass at Fighters of Doom*! Damn … the batteries are getting low … I hope Mom doesn't find out I cheated on my math test …*

I leap up as quickly as I can, but I still feel sullied. "Get away from me!" I yell. My voice carries across the room, but no one hears me. I bite my lip, stumbling away from the couch where Terry occupies my old spot — Terrence Phillip Jones, but he goes by Terry. He's in third grade, and he loves peanut butter and banana sandwiches, and —

I'm Emma, not Terry. Emma! I try to shake free of the otherness of his person, his being, even though I know it usually takes a few minutes until I feel like myself again. I shudder and move back to my previous post at the shelf, but even that's not safe because Terry's two brothers, who for that brief moment I knew just as well as Terry does —

… Jack and Jerry … twins, both evil … they put dog shit in my bed the other night, and gave me a wedgie on the bus last Tuesday …

— round the corner, arguing full steam. I duck out of their way just in time to avoid being touched again. I hate this! I scratch my head with both hands, raking my scalp with my nails as I try to force the last bits of Terry's mind out of my own, his thoughts, his memories, his dreams lingering in mine like footsteps in wet grass.

I retreat to the other side of the store and curl up in a little ball on the checkered couch, the comfortable couch, the one I sit on when it's the middle of the night and I wish with all my might that I could go home. I hear the raindrops from outside, but in my mind the fire crackles in the hearth, warming our little house. Mama puts the kettle on. Papa says to me, in his stern Papa voice, "Fetch some more wood, Emma, my lass." Freddie giggles, running the toy train Papa carved for him over the wide pine planks of the floor. Lizzie sits in the rocking chair, head bent over her cross-stitch.

Although they are vivid in my memory, I know those days are gone forever. I smack the soft arm of the sofa with my fist, but my intangibility keeps me from having the satisfaction of feeling the stuffing give.

My home is gone. Even if our house is still there, my family isn't. My parents, my sister, my brother … They're all dead, and have been for years and years and years. I was murdered in 1873, when Lizzie was fifteen, and Freddie was five. Even if they both lived to be a hundred they've been dead for a long, long time.

I lay my head on the back of the couch, the mustiness of the fabric familiar, full of my invisible tears.

~~~~~

After a while I drag myself up and wander back to the front window. The woman with the pointed shoes is on the other side of the street, next to the streetlight by the bookstore. She's without her companion, and appears a bit more bedraggled, but at least she's managed to find an umbrella. She paces back and forth, making one call after another on her cell phone. I have no idea what's wrong, but I entertain myself by coming up with stories. Maybe she's supposed to meet someone who's late? Maybe the man she was with earlier was her boyfriend, or her husband, and she's angry with him? Perhaps she just lost her job *and* she's angry with her husband? I craft my imaginary scenarios one by one, discarding each when I think of something new.

The store is pretty quiet. Vicki and Stacia are behind the counter — they're the only ones working right now. Stacia is short and has long, amazingly straight blonde hair. Vicki has dark brown hair and olive-toned skin. I heard her say once that she's part Italian and part Seminole, which I guess is a kind of Indian. The Indians who lived here when I was alive were mostly Arapaho and Cheyenne, but I've never heard mention of Seminole. Vicki and Stacia are both in their early twenties, which technically makes them older than me, although after being dead for a while, age doesn't seem all that relevant. Would I be different now if I'd been older when I died? Or if I'd been younger?

I ponder this for the millionth time while I watch Vicki ring up a customer. She's working here while she gets her nursing degree. Stacia doesn't think she's smart enough to go to college, so she's working here because she doesn't know what else to do. I know this from listening to them, not from touching them.

There are a few other people in the store — not many, but it should pick up in a bit. I look forward to the busier times. I have to work harder to avoid touching anyone, but having more people around temporarily alleviates the dullness. Edward is here, of course. He's here just about every day, although he hardly ever rents a movie. He's in his mid-thirties, or at least I think he is. It's hard to tell because I've never seen him take off his sunglasses, regardless of what time of day it is. He's a heavyset, unsavory-looking man who rides a Harley and wears leather and chains. He clearly fancies Stacia. He prowls around the store in those heavy leather boots, pretending to look at movies, but I can tell he's always got one eye on the counter.

There's also the pale girl I saw earlier. She's been pacing up and down the aisles for a while. She seems vaguely familiar. I spent most of the morning watching people through the front window, so perhaps I saw her pass by outside. She's quite pretty, even with that serious look on her face, which makes it odd that Edward hasn't noticed her, especially since she just walked by him. He's probably too focused on Stacia. I think he's figured out her work schedule, because he's almost always here when she's working.

I turn back to the window just in time to see the woman across the street get into a car and slam the door; the car speeds away, tires squealing. Yet another snippet of someone else's life, another mystery for me to wonder about, since I have no life of my own.

I start walking along the wall, trailing my fingers across it. Might as well do my rounds now. Long ago I developed a habit of traversing the boundaries at least once a day. I usually start by tracing them on the ground floor, then the second story. I check out the basement sometimes. I don't like to go down there, but I make myself just in case a way out miraculously appears. I so hate going down there. I remember every detail of my old prison, even though it doesn't exist now; the chill of the stone wall underneath my fingers, the earthy scent of the dirt floor, the sound of his feet stomping on the wooden boards above me.

The bells on the front door jingle and I pause, my fingertips still touching the wall. I lean around the shelves and peek over at the counter, hoping that Matt has come in, even though he's not supposed to be working tonight. It's not Matt, unfortunately, just a balding, middle-aged man. I sure wish it had been Matt instead. There's something about him, something irresistibly captivating. I follow him around the store when he's here, admiring him, watching every move he makes, even when he's sitting at the counter doing nothing at all. I love listening to his voice, the tones warm and rich and charming no matter what he's saying. I know it's ridiculous. He'll never even be aware of my existence. But I can't help but feel happy when he's around, and that's so unusual that I've given myself license to enjoy it.

The pale girl glanced up when the door opened, but now she's back to pacing the aisles. At least I think that's what she's doing. She doesn't seem to be reading the movie titles; she's just walking up and down the aisles. She must have gone through them all several times by now. I watch with absent-minded curiosity as she proceeds methodically through the store, row by row, then I move out of her path right before she reaches me.

She stops and looks directly at me, which is, of course, pure coincidence because there's no way she can see me. Her lashes are long and full, her eyes a golden-brown with little flecks of green; the exact same color Lizzie's eyes were. Her long hair is lovely, a rich, warm brown with blonde streaks. It's very pretty, although the blonde bits look a little too evenly spaced to be natural. These days most of the girls color their hair, or else they have something pierced or maybe tattooed. It all seems awfully foolish to me, but apparently this sort of thing is the fashion.

I step to the side, to her left, and her eyes follow me. They can't, but they do. It's almost as though she really does see me. I gawk at her for a minute.

"Would you please not stare at me like that?" she asks.

There's a loud ringing in my ears, as if I have just been smacked on the head. She's looking directly at me. There's no one else here. She *has* to be looking at me. She's talking to *me*.

No one has ever seen me, not once in all these years. Yet clearly she does.

I stare at her, my mouth hanging open.

She makes a small, exasperated sound, rolls her eyes, then spins around and marches off.

My entire body is frozen solid. *She saw me.* I stand there, thunderstruck, as she turns the corner of the nearest aisle and is gone from my sight.

My feet feel as though they've grown roots and will never again be willing to move. No one has seen me — and no one has spoken to me — for the 130 years since my death in 1873. But she did! I sway back and forth slightly, staring at the spot where I last saw her. There's a strange thumping in my chest, and my entire body is buzzing like the bells of an alarm clock.

I rip my feet from their moorings and rush around the corner after her, filled with a desperate need to find her, to follow her — to be seen by her.

The aisle is empty.

I dash to the end of the aisle, turning frantically from left to right. The girl is nowhere to be seen. *Where is she?* My heart pounds madly away. I lunge to my left and peer down the next row over, but she's not there. I run from row to row as fast as I can, my steps so unsteady I have to put out a hand to catch myself as I whip around the end of each shelf to see yet another empty aisle. *She saw me!* I race up the stairs and search the rooms on the second floor, barely avoiding colliding into a man in the Independent Films section. *Where is she?* I head back down the steps, pausing only to look across the main room, but I don't see her. I sprint through each aisle, one after another, dodging the few living people who are in the store at this time of day. Finally I come to a halt by the front window. I'm filled with so much energy that I feel I could fly, but I don't know what to do. Where did she go?

I lean my back against the wall and sink to the floor, hugging my knees to my chest.

I sit there until my breathing slows. Could I have imagined her? Maybe, after all these years, I'm finally going crazy? I sigh, a deep, mighty sigh, and pull myself to my feet, one hand pressed against the wall for balance. I feel unaccountably heavy, as if I've suddenly gained a thousand pounds. It's a tremendous effort just to stand up.

She couldn't have seen me. No one can.

I stumble blindly across the room, passing row after row of movies, barely managing to keep out of the way of the customers roaming the store. My steps are as slow as an elephant's. I pause, my fingertips resting on the wall, and look through the doorway into the next room.

She's standing by Horror.

I can't tear my eyes from her face. She's looking right at me — *right at me*. Her hands are on her hips, and her brow is furrowed. She can't see me, she can't! But clearly she does. She must be a ghost too. That's why Edward wasn't watching her.

"Stop staring at me!" she demands. Her eyes narrow, and her hands clench into fists. My legs feel all quavery, as though they might give way.

"You're staring at me, too." My voice sounds dull and flat. Since my death I've spoken to myself, and I've said things to the living, knowing no one can hear me no matter how desperately I wish they could. But now that I'm speaking to someone who *can* hear me I sound hollow, like an echo instead of the original, as if I've suddenly become even less real.

"You were staring first."

The first time another person has spoken to me since my death and we're arguing with each other. I don't know what to say to her. There are so many things to say, to ask. I open my mouth, but my tongue is all twisted in knots. I can't let her leave again. I have to say something.

"Are you —" I stop and clear my throat again. "Are you a ghost?" My chest tightens as I hear my voice break a little.

Her lips purse, and one eyebrow lifts slightly. "What are you talking about?" She fiddles with her necklace, a gold chain with a single diamond. There's a small mole on her left cheek. She's not wearing earrings, but there are tiny holes in her ears so I can tell her ears are pierced. She seems so *real*.

I take a step toward her, drawn as if by a magnet. She has to be a ghost. No one has *ever* seen me in all the years I've been stuck here. And now … I swallow and sidle through the doorway. Now I'm not alone — now I'll never be alone again!

But how can she not know she's dead? Perhaps she died in her sleep? I feel suddenly sorry for her, sorry for someone lost like I am, but who doesn't yet realize that she's lost.

"I'm a ghost," I say softly. "If you can see me, then you must be one too." The poor girl. Although at least I'll be able to explain things about being a ghost to her.

She narrows her eyes. "That's ridiculous. I'm not dead. And you aren't either." She sounds undaunted, as if she's not only sure that she's not a ghost, but she's also convinced that I'm insane. She takes a step back and looks around. "Are you okay? Are you with someone? Maybe I should get you some help."

I open my mouth, then realize I don't know how to respond to her. She marches off to the counter where Stacia sits painting her nails. I follow, feeling my heart thump madly away, hopeful that I won't be alone any more, yet guilty for wishing this existence on someone else. She has to be a ghost. She just *has* to be.

"Hello? Does anyone know this woman? She —" The girl glances at me, then turns back to Stacia. "I think she might be lost." I suppose that's a diplomatic way to put it. I expected her to say I was crazy.

Stacia holds out her right hand, her bright red nails glistening in the fluorescent light; the lurid color looks like blood. She turns her hand from side to side, shakes her head, and bends to touch one of them up, biting her lower lip as she concentrates on running the brush over her fingernail. The acrid scent of the polish makes my nose tingle; it doesn't seem to bother Stacia.

"Excuse me," the pale girl says. She leans over the counter — there's no way Stacia can miss her. "I said, excuse me!" Her tone is sharp. Stacia puts the brush back in the bottle, screws the lid on tight, then examines her handiwork.

The other girl has to be a ghost, then. Although it's peculiar that she doesn't *know* she is. Can a person die and not notice it?

I clear my throat, which feels as though a million frogs are caught in it.

"She can't see you."

The girl glares at me.

"Of course she can. She's just being rude." She turns back to Stacia. "Hello, hello? Hey you!" She waves her hand in front of Stacia's face.

Stacia blows on her nails, then smiles and holds her hands up, all ten fingers splayed out. "Hey, Vicki, I have a great idea for the party!"

I see Edward out of the corner of my eye; he's leaning against Action and Adventure, pretending to read the back cover of a movie, but it's obvious he's really ogling Stacia.

"Yeah? Hold on a minute." Vicki stomps down from the second floor, lugging a tall stack of DVDs. "I hate when people put the cases back out of order!" As she walks across the room she trips and several of the movies fly on the carpet in front of the counter, right in front of us.

The ghost girl makes a face at Stacia, then looks at Vicki. "Could someone please help me?" she snaps.

Vicki sets what is left of the stack of movies on the counter and bends over to pick up the others. "So what's your idea?" I step to the side, out of her way. The other girl doesn't move.

"We should dress up like characters from '80s movies!" Stacia replies, then squints at her fingernails.

"What the hell is wrong with you people?" the girl yells, throwing her hands up in the air. She focuses on the stack of movies, clenches her jaw, then thrusts a fist at it. Her fist stops sharp at the edge of the stack, which remains as firm as a stone wall. She freezes, staring at her hand, then begins to poke at the cases with a finger. They don't move.

"That's a great idea!" Vicki replies. She's looking at Stacia through the pale girl, who is staring at her hands as though she's never seen them before. Vicki drops the rest of the movies on the counter next to the first stack. The plastic cases clatter harshly on the Formica.

"What's going on?" the other ghost mutters. She pivots, moving as if she's in slow motion, her eyes unfocused. She stops as she notices a pen that has fallen to the floor, and squats down to pick it up. Without success.

I glance back at Vicki and Stacia. My innards feel as if they're all twisted around each other. They can't see this other girl; they really can't. She *is* a ghost.

She stands up. She doesn't *look* like a ghost. She looks as real as Vicki does. A little whiter, perhaps, but not in a ghostly way. More like someone who hasn't seen the sun for a while.

For the first time since I died there's someone who can see me, who can hear me. Someone who knows I exist.

The ghost girl shakes her head, her hazel eyes wet. She blinks. "I don't understand," she mutters. She moves a few feet away from the counter, her lower lip trembling as she watches Vicki and Stacia. They chatter away, their voices humming like the sound of a movie playing in the background. I take a step toward her, then stop when I realize my hand is outstretched. I don't know what will happen if I touch her. Will I become her, like I do with the living?

The bells jingle as someone enters the store. I drop my hand, hoping the other girl didn't notice. She'd surely think me mad if I tried to explain. But I could explain, if I wanted to — and she'd hear me. *I'm not alone!*

The ghost girl starts plodding toward the front of the building, her head hanging down low. I follow and realize I want to skip, to jump. I'm still dead, but I feel almost as though I'm alive. I force myself to move at a normal pace as I trail after her, my feet filled with an energy I didn't know they had. She reaches the window, and I stop a few feet away. *I'm not alone anymore!*

"Oh my God. They — they didn't see me, they really didn't. Why? Why can't they see me?" She looks down at the windowsill and runs a finger across the painted wood, the once-smooth surface now cracked and worn with age.

I take a deep breath, my glee suddenly replaced by solemnity. Through the window I see the sky has cleared and the moon has appeared, a slim, white sliver fighting to outshine the light of the city below. I feel as if I've turned to lead, my energy gone. What can I tell her? I have no comfort to offer, no solace to share. She's stuck here, now, with me. Forever.

I open my mouth again, then close it without speaking. I am suddenly very aware of my hands. I don't know what to do with them, so I clasp them together until they hurt. She closes her eyes, the darkness of her long lashes pronounced against her pale skin.

"I don't understand. This doesn't make any sense. If I'm dead, why don't I remember dying?" Her hands are balled into fists so tight that the outline of her collarbone is visible through her sweater. She slams a fist against the wall, and I flinch even though the blow makes no sound. "I don't want to be dead!"

"I'm sorry. I don't understand either." *I* remember dying. I remember the horrible things he did to me, the pain, the fear, the anger, the hatred, the hope … And then the absence of everything, both welcome and terrible. I remember everything. With perfect clarity.

She presses her forehead against the wall, hiding her face in her hands. We stand there in silence, me unsure what to say, unable to give comfort, her grappling with the change in her world. This poor girl! I haven't spoken with someone for so long, and now I have a companion, but it's not a situation I would have chosen. Why not someone who'd been a ghost for a while?

This girl doesn't seem to remember her death, so maybe she was lucky and it wasn't awful like mine. But death is still death.

Without thinking, I reach my hand out to her again, then jerk it back to my chest. I want to touch her; I want to hug her, to console her like I would have Lizzie. But I can't do it, I just can't touch anyone. It's too horrible.

"What's your name?" I ask instead. My voice trembles a little. I stand up straight. I have to be strong for her. I've been dead for a long, long time, but this girl must have just died. I don't know what I can do, but I'd like to help her. I'd like to make her feel better. If I can.

She uncovers her face, which is now not pale, but pink and blotchy, her skin wet from her tears. "What?"

"I'm Emma." It's strange to say my name aloud after so many, many years.

"Ashley," she whispers. We stand there for a moment, the silence loud and awkward.

"Hey, wait a minute." Her eyes grow wide, and she perks up, energized. "What day is today?"

Ashley dashes back to the counter, with me trailing close behind. She leans over the counter and looks past Stacia, who stands with her arms crossed while Vicki talks with a freckled fellow near the front door. He seems familiar somehow — perhaps I saw him in the store on another day, or maybe watched him walk by outside. I smile as I think about how wonderful it's going to be to have someone else here. Someone to watch the living with me, someone to keep me company at night when it rains and I'm scared. Someone to talk to. Someone to be my friend.

Ashley leans over the countertop and squints at the computer screen, then turns to face me, her smile so radiant I can feel my own lips curving up.

"It's Thursday!" she declares. She tosses her long hair over her shoulder. "I was alive *yesterday*! I went to school and to volleyball practice and —" She rubs her left temple, scrunching up her eyes for a moment.

I try, unsuccessfully, to recall what volleyball is.

"That's all I remember." Her tone softens, and she slumps. "I remember leaving practice, but — but —" She stares at the floor.

I wish I could say something to help her, but of course there's no way for me to know anything about her death. I was here all day yesterday, as I always am; I spent most of last night on the second floor, reminiscing about home.

"I'm going to find out what happened," she announces, straightening her shoulders.

Find out? I watch, perplexed, as Ashley marches to the door and reaches her hand out to open it, then jerks back when her hand passes through the frame.

"Wait —" I hear myself whisper. What is she doing? "Ashley, Ashley, don't —" My voice is soft as a kitten's meow. She glances at me and grins, then takes a deep breath and leaps through the door.

"No!"

My chest feels as if something has been ripped out of it — where is she going? She's leaving, leaving me here alone!

I dash to the door and watch her through the glass, my hands pressed flat against its coldness. She's running down the street, and is already much further away than I can go! I throw myself through the door and plunge onto the porch —

— and then I slam into my wall, the invisible wall of the house I was murdered in. I slump to my knees, my body pressed against my ever-present barrier, my fingers sliding down the old wooden wall I can feel but can't see. There's a pain, a horrible, tight awfulness, all the way from my neck down to my stomach. Why was she able to leave the building? Why am I trapped here? Why did she leave me here — *alone?*

Ashley seems to grow smaller as she moves farther away, her body casting no shadow in spite of the streetlamp. She sprints around the corner by the shoe shop and is gone. If only I could follow her! If only I could help her! If only —

I scream, pounding on the wall with my fists, hammering its implacable surface over and over. Tears run down my cheeks, falling off my face and vanishing like the nothingness that they are. But the wall that isn't there continues to persist in its solidity for me, and so I remain, trapped as always within its boundaries.

I sink to my knees and sit there for a long time, my tears drying while I ignore the exhaust fumes tickling my nose, the cars moving in and out of the parking lot, the people walking up and down the street, and in and out of the store, talking, shopping, *living.*

After a while I stand up, turn my back to the night, and head inside, into the fluorescence.

I hope Ashley finds out what she needs to know. I hope it's something good, as good as it can be, considering. I hope —

I hope she comes back.

Two

I've been lonely for so long the emptiness has become a familiar, muted ache, but now I feel it sharp in my chest, like a thousand tiny knives stabbing into me. I stomp my feet as I walk the boundaries on the first and second floors, circling round and round the store, until more customers come in and I get tired of having to continually work to avoid touching them. I stare out the pane of glass next to the door to the parking lot, down at the street corner where I last saw Ashley.

Ashley reminds me an awful lot of Lizzie, maybe because she looks to be about fifteen, the age Lizzie was when I died. Why is she not tied to wherever she died, like I am? Losing my life would have been easier if I had not been yoked to the place of my death — wouldn't it? Would it really have been easier if I could have watched my parents grow old, if I could have seen my brother and sister grow up and have children of their own, my nieces and nephews? I'll never know. I'll never find out what happened to any of my family. For all I know Ashley could even be one of my great-great nieces.

Although ... I swallow, aware of a huge lump in my throat, even though I know my throat turned to dust long ago. If Ashley comes back, maybe she can help me find a way out. *She* can leave the building, even though it makes no sense that she should be able to when I can't. No sense at all.

I shake my head. This is ridiculous. Without being able to interact with the physical world, without looking through records and papers that Ashley won't be able to do no matter what place she can go to, there's no way she'd be able to learn anything. And what would I gain anyway? Peace of mind? Knowing that my sister didn't die in childbirth? Learning that my brother didn't become a cowboy, but ran off and joined the circus instead? I shudder, feeling like a spider just crawled across my shoulders. What if Lizzie *did* die in childbirth? Do I really want to know that?

Perhaps the past should be left in the past, my questions and curiosities left unanswered.

Besides, Ashley might not come back.

I poke at the edge of the nearest shelf, my finger tapping soundlessly against the wood. Maybe she's found out what happened to herself and isn't even a ghost anymore. Maybe *her* unfinished business was learning how she died.

I clench my fists as my body is filled with a sudden, blinding heat. *I* want to leave. *I* want to move on to the next place, wherever it is, whatever it is. I want *out* of this torturous, tedious existence!

I close my eyes, angry, angrier than I've been for years and years —

— then everything stops as someone steps into me. It's Edward, awful, horrible Edward.

… Her hair is beautiful, so long and bright and shiny, as if it was made from millions of tiny silken threads. She'd look spectacular on a bike. On my bike. Wearing nothing but heels and a black lace bra that barely restrained those lovely tits, her wrists tied behind her back. Oh, baby. I'd run my hands over them, my fingers tracing the soft curve underneath each one, so perfect and smooth. She'd make little sounds, soft moans, begging me to stop while her nipples hardened under my touch. I'd take my tongue and —

I spring out of him and flatten myself against the wall, my breath catching as I pull as far away from him as I can. I'd go *through* the wall if I could, but it parallels the old wall, and that barrier is as firm as ever. I feel as though I've been spun around in circles, then punched in the stomach. My wrists ache something fierce, as if they were still bound by the rope my captor had used. The images from Edward's mind linger in mine, soiling my thoughts like streaks of mud splashed on a fresh, clean skirt.

Edward shivers, momentarily cold from my presence even in his leather jacket. Good! That's what he gets for touching me! I grin even though my legs are quivering.

If I wasn't a ghost I think I might vomit. I press my hand on my belly, trying to will the nausea away, then squeeze past him, careful not to get too close. I stumble toward the corner where the checkered couch beckons, its familiar worn cushions a warm and welcoming haven. I pause at the end of the aisle and glance back at Edward. He's eyeing a slender blonde girl who just walked in; she looks like she's around Ashley's age. For a split second I smell damp, wet earth. I shudder, then the scent is gone, replaced by the familiar mustiness of the old building. I swallow and turn around to see someone sitting on the couch that was empty a second ago.

Ashley! Ashley's back!

"Where did you come from?" I wheel around, but all I see is the intersection of the two aisles, empty except for disgusting, leather-clad Edward. She must have come through the wall! There's no way she could have been in the store and snuck by me that quickly. But she's back. She's back! My glee wipes away the residue left by Edward's touch.

"Oh, hi, Emma," she replies, her voice airy. "I've been sitting here for a while." She waves a hand, as if this makes sense.

"No you haven't." She certainly wasn't there a minute ago, so why would she claim she was? "But I'm *so* glad you're back!"

"Yes, yes, I was. I think." Her brow wrinkles slightly. "But I don't remember how I got here. I was at my mom's house, and — and now I'm here." She nibbles on a nail. I wait for her to say something else, but apparently that's it.

How could she not know how she got here? I don't believe her, although there's no reason I can think of for her to be lying. I sit down on the sofa and tuck my feet underneath me, being careful not to bump into her.

"Did you find out anything about —" I pause, uncertain of how to put it politely. What's a nice way to ask someone if they discovered how they died?

"Sort of," she replies, unfazed by the topic. She selects a small chunk of her hair and begins to plait it while she stares off into space. "I seem to be missing."

"Missing?" I repeat, my voice louder than I intended it to be. She's dead, and no one knows how — or where — or why? In a way that could be worse than learning about how you died. Not that dying and being a ghost isn't awful, but I know what happened to me. Although — maybe that's not really such a great thing to remember, considering the circumstances of my death. I put my hand to my neck and rub my skin. Even after all these years I remember exactly how it felt; the coarse fibers digging into my flesh, trying desperately to breathe while he pulled the rope tighter and tighter.

Ignorance might be frustrating, but at least I'd lack the memories I have of dying.

"Yeah, well, whatever," she mutters, and starts on another braid. We sit in silence. I feel as though I should say something, but I don't know what. I'm not used to having anyone around, much less someone who has just died and is upset about it. Was she murdered? Did she have a heart attack? She's awfully young for that sort of thing to happen, but you never know. I'm tempted to braid my own hair to distract myself from our uncomfortable silence.

"Maybe — " I start, then pause. I want to make her feel better. I'd like to say something nice — but what can I say? "Maybe it's better to not know," bursts out of me. I clasp my hands together in my lap, my fingers tight around one another. She must have been murdered. That's the most likely scenario. *The rope was tight around my neck, it couldn't get any tighter — it couldn't! He had to stop, he had to let me go. He had to.* I realize I'm gripping so hard my knuckles are white.

Ashley glowers at me. "No, it's not. If I'm dead I have the right to know what happened. It's not fair for me not to know, it's *not fair*." Her fingers twist away, each little braid beginning to loosen as soon as she releases it to start on the next one. "*You know how you died, don't you?*"

I stare at the arm of the sofa, noticing — for the millionth time — how the checkered pattern isn't made up of black and white fibers, but black and charcoal and gray and white.

"Yes." I run my finger over the multi-colored squares. There's a small rip on the edge of the cushion.

"Well, isn't it better to *know*? Maybe it wasn't fun to die, I mean," She squirms a bit in her seat and looks at the floor. "I'm sure it sucked. But at least you don't have to *wonder*."

That's certainly true.

I glance back at Ashley; remnants of tiny braids, all partially unraveled, are scattered through her hair. "I expect you're right. I hope you find out what happened."

A couple of children run by, a boy and a girl, both maybe Freddie's age. The boy is chasing the girl, and they're giggling like mad. Ashley glares at the pair as they pass.

"It was probably my brother," she growls. "He's been angry because Dad is buying *me* a car, but Scott didn't get one because he didn't keep his grades up."

"Your brother wouldn't murder you." I don't really know that he wouldn't, but it seems unlikely. She crosses her arms and wrinkles her nose. I hadn't noticed before, but she has a light sprinkling of freckles across the bridge, just like Lizzie did.

"Do — do you remember *anything* about what happened yesterday? After volleyball?"

"No, I don't remember a damn thing." She gets up and starts to pace in front of the couch. "I went to practice, then Savannah was going to give me a ride home. She already has a car." She stomps back and forth, back and forth, the thumping of her feet soundless on the thin carpet. "I was talking with Melanie, then I went outside to meet Savannah. She didn't want to be around Melanie because Melanie borrowed a book from her and lost it and won't buy her a new one. Which is pretty rude, but I think Melanie's brother is really cute." She waves an arm, presumably to emphasize just how cute he is.

"But when I got outside, her car was gone. She was supposed to wait for me — she said she would be there. But she wasn't. The next thing I remember is walking around this store. I have no idea how I got here."

Ashley stops suddenly, her eyes fixed on something across the room. I glance in that direction, but from my position on the sofa I can't see what she's looking at. She stands on her toes, craning her neck to peer over the shelves.

"There she is, that *bitch*!" She marches off in pursuit.

I trot after her and catch up in Comedy. She's scowling at the blonde girl Edward was looking at earlier. Ashley points at the blonde and proclaims, "It's *her* fault! *She's* the reason I'm dead!"

I inspect the girl, who seems normal enough. She's wearing jeans, a fuzzy lavender sweater, and matching lavender boots with heels that have to be at least three inches tall. It's fascinating that someone might actually buy a pair of purple shoes just to coordinate with a sweater.

"*She* murdered you?" This girl looks friendly and pleasant, not like a murderer — although you can't necessarily tell, I suppose. And even in the movies the people who appear to be innocent are occasionally ruthless killers. My murderer was all scraggly and mean and unkempt, but he could have looked like Mr. Smit, who ran the general store in town. You just never know.

"No, of course not!" Ashley rolls her eyes. "This is Savannah, my best friend. She was going to give me a ride home, and she wasn't there. Whatever happened to me must have happened because she left without me. Because —" Her breath catches.

Savannah picks up a movie and turns it over to read the back cover. She tucks a strand of fine blonde hair behind her left ear; her diamond earring sparkles as it reflects the fluorescent light. Her eye shadow is exactly the same color as her sweater and her boots. She smells like vanilla.

Ashley digs a toe into the carpet and continues, her voice almost a whisper.

"She must not really like me. She was my friend, and she forgot me." I meet Ashley's gaze as a tear trickles down her cheek.

"She *forgot* me and someone killed me." Ashley sniffles, then coughs as she chokes back a sob.

I'm sure that isn't what happened. Ashley said Savannah is her best friend, and friends don't forget each other. If Savannah had left without Ashley there must have been some reason — right? Would I have ever intentionally left a friend of mine behind? No. Absolutely not.

Although … The first time Ned offered to walk me home I left without even telling my girlfriend Beverly. I knew Bev would figure it out. She — and pretty much everyone else —

teased me mercilessly for weeks afterward, but it was worth the harassment. I remember how special I felt, how warm and happy it made me inside when Ned offered to carry my books, and how a tingle ran up my arm when I handed them to him and his hand brushed against mine.

But what if something had happened to Beverly because I'd left her to walk home alone? What if it had been Lizzie instead? I feel a cold, hard knot in my middle. I'm sure Savannah did something similar — she must have!

There's one thing I can do to help Ashley. I cringe inside. It's too hard, too awful! But Ashley is my friend. More my potential friend, I suppose, but also my only chance at having a friend in over a hundred years. I can't stand the thought of having Ashley around for all eternity, knowing that I could have made her feel better and knowing that I chose not to help her because it would have been unpleasant for me — and unpleasant for only a short time at that. A few seconds, that's all it would be. That's nothing compared to the length of time I've been a ghost.

I clasp my hands together and try to steel myself to touch Savannah. My chest tightens and my legs won't move. I've never entered another person intentionally. I can't do it, I just can't!

"Hold on," I hear myself say. I scrunch up my face, take a deep breath, and step forward.

Into Savannah's world.

… God-fucking-dammit … I can't believe my nail broke … just got my manicure on Sunday … now I have to go back to the spa and complain … Fuck … I'm starving … no way was I going

to eat anything after Frances started yelling at Dad … She's right, too … Dad is having another affair … Goddamn lying bastard …

My mind is crowded with her thoughts, her memories. My feet feel funny, and I realize they're not mine — they're Savannah's feet, squashed into those ridiculous high-heeled boots. I can't even feel my own body anymore. I want to move, I want to get away, to get *out* of Savannah's mind!

But I have to stay; I have to see if she knows anything about Ashley. Please, oh please let her think about Ashley!

… I don't know why my father has to be such a loser … all my friends have normal families … if their parents aren't happy they just get divorced … Why doesn't Dad just divorce Frances? Why doesn't she just divorce him? … God, I miss Mom …

I feel lost, submerged, as if my soul is being squashed by Savannah's. And she isn't aware of it at all. She has no idea I'm here. Why isn't she thinking about Ashley?

I watch as my — her — fingers reach out and pick up another movie. Her nail polish seems so wrong, so unnatural, but I find myself admiring it nonetheless. Is that my admiration or Savannah's? I can no longer tell. I stare at the back of the movie, looking through Savannah's eyes, but I can't read anything because she isn't focusing on the text.

I can't take this any more, I can't do this, I can't I can't I can't …

… Dad promised he wouldn't cheat anymore … He told me we'd be a normal family again … as normal as possible, that is … But he lied, just like all the other times. I saw him with some woman yesterday when I was driving around looking for Ashley … Fuck. Fucking liar … Dammit, Ashley, where the fuck are you? …

The police said maybe she ran away, but she wouldn't ... I would, though ... I just don't know where to go ... I wish I'd told Ashley about Dad. I want to, I really want to tell her ... not that stupid psychiatrist Frances and Dad are making me go to ... he knows about Dad, I can tell from the questions he asks me ... but I'm not going to talk about it ... not to him ... not to anyone ... I should be happy that Dad is having another affair because he'll be off with her and the house will be quiet for a change ... I hope ... Goddammit, where is Ashley? I'm so worried about her ... who is that disgusting old man at the end of the aisle? He's watching me ... what a creep ...

I can't see the man watching her, but I know it's Edward; I can see his image in her memory. Her indignation is my indignation, her frustration with her psychiatrist — a balding, well-meaning, but totally uncool man — is my frustration. Her anger and disgust at her father for his many infidelities are now mine as well.

I feel less and less like *me*.

... If some asshole hadn't put poured a fucking can of paint on my car I would have been there on time to pick up Ashley ... was she kidnapped? ... no, she's fine. Ashley is fine. She's just gone off somewhere ... She's okay. She's okay and she'll show up soon ... she will ... God it's bright in here ... I can't waste much more time in this stupid store before I'm going to have to go back home ... Dad has probably gone to see his stupid, fucking girlfriend ... Frances is probably drunk again —

I step back, out of Savannah, and rub my arms. I keep moving backward, away from her, until I bump into the rack of movies behind me. I should make sure no one else is nearby — I can't touch another person, especially after that! I blink to clear my vision, then notice Ashley, who is staring at me as if I've sprouted horns.

"What did you do?"

She reaches out to touch my shoulder, then draws her hand back. We both move aside as Savannah heads down the aisle. She's shivering, thanks to my touch, but otherwise seems oblivious to what just happened.

I rub my eyes, then run my fingers through my hair, pulling the ends of my hair — *hard!* — so I can feel something different. Something of *me*.

"Savannah didn't forget you. Her, uh." My tongue feels thick and heavy, and so does my brain, as if my thoughts had turned to syrup.

"Sarah. My sister. Fu — um." I stop before my lips can complete the word, a word I've never before uttered, and shudder. "Someone poured hot pink paint all over her car."

I twist my head from side to side, wishing I could shake loose the fragments of Savannah that are still inside of me. The scent of vanilla remains in my mind even though my nose can no longer smell it.

"You read her mind?"

"Yeah, kinda." The sloppy speech rolls smoothly off my tongue. I dig my unpolished fingernails into my palms.

Becoming a person for a second is like mind reading, although I've always imagined reading someone's mind to be a significantly less overpowering activity. I open my mouth, then close it. I've never stayed inside a person for that long, not intentionally, at least. I don't feel like myself, nor like Savannah, either. I peer down the aisle at Savannah. She picks up a movie, glances at it, then sets it down and picks up another. I know she's not really looking at any of them.

"What happened to her mother?" I ask. My Savannah memories are fading, but I'm quite clear that something bad happened to her mother. I'm filled with a sudden desire, powerfully strong, to see my own.

Ashley is far too focused to answer my question.

"How did you do that? You walked into her, and then it was like you were sort of inside of her! But I could still see you. And her." She holds her breath for a moment, then lets it out in a burst of words. "Does she know what happened to me?"

"No, she doesn't." Ashley sags, like a balloon losing air. "But she is really worried about you."

I watch Savannah, who has wandered down to the end of the aisle, still aimlessly looking at movies to distract herself from her worries about Ashley and her many frustrations with her father. She just happened to walk by this store — it's a coincidence that this is where Ashley, the ghost Ashley, is. I feel sorry for Savannah, sorry that she's scared about her friend, sorry that she has such a bad man for a father. I wish I could help both her *and* Ashley.

Ashley looks down at her feet and her shoulders droop.

"I'm worried about me too."

We stand there for a moment, then she turns and heads after Savannah, pacing the other girl like a shadow. I take a deep breath, then follow, my steps slow, and catch up to them at the front of the store. Ashley is leaning against the counter, watching Savannah as she pretends to browse the used DVDs on sale.

"She doesn't *seem* worried about me," Ashley mutters.

"What do you want her to do? For all she knows you ran away." I cross my arms, feeling oddly protective of Savannah. "Besides, she's used to hiding how she feels."

Ashley eyes her friend, her face suspicious. "She doesn't hide anything from me. Does she?"

"She thinks of you as her best friend, so stop fretting." I snap. I hoist myself onto the counter and sit back against the wall.

Ashley looks contrite. "I'm sorry. I — I just don't really like being … being dead."

We watch Savannah pick up movie after movie. She looks so calm on the outside, but on the inside I know she's scared — scared for Ashley and scared to go home.

A deep, male voice coughs nearby, the harsh sound interrupting my thoughts. I look up, my breath catching at the familiar sight of Matt's golden curls as he walks past the end of the aisle. I hear him chuckle, a warm, rumbling laugh that causes me to grin even though I don't know what he's amused by. What is he doing here? He isn't scheduled to work tonight; this is the evening he has photography class.

The cough sounds again, and I turn toward it to see someone peeking around the end of the Comedy aisle, watching Savannah.

Edward's mirrored sunglasses reflect the fluorescent light.

Three

When did you die?" Ashley asks me. We're sitting on the checkered couch watching a wrinkled, steel-haired woman browse the shelves. The collection in the basket on her walker contains a few bags of popcorn, a comedy, and a pornographic film. The woman keeps peeking in the basket to make sure that the other movies are covering the pornographic one. She doesn't seem to realize that the title on the side of the DVD case is visible through the wire mesh of the basket.

"Are you from around here? How did *you* die?" She clears her throat. "That isn't too rude to ask, is it?"

I smile. "No, it's not rude." It might be rude to another ghost, but as I've never met another ghost except for Ashley we might as well make up our own standards of propriety.

" My house is — was — a few miles away." It might still be there, for all I know. Ashley tilts her head, staring at me like a bird watching a worm. I'm sure she has no idea how far a mile was in my time. "I, uh, died in 1873."

"No way!" She squirms around on the couch. "That is so cool! Did you get scarlet fever? I read a book once where everyone got scarlet fever and then died. Well —" she pauses. "Not all of them died. But it was set in the 1800s. Did that happen to you?"

I press against the arm of the couch, a little overwhelmed. This much enthusiasm would be unnerving even if we weren't discussing my death. I'm not used to conversing with other people any more.

"No, I was murdered."

The word falls off my tongue with ease. I was murdered. It's amazing how I can say that so effortlessly when I've spent so much time trying not to remember it.

"Really?" Ashley's eyes are big. "Wow. Do you think I was, too?"

"I certainly hope not." Although given what she's told me, murder does seem like a possibility. I stretch my legs straight out in front of me and stare at my feet.

"Hey!" My head jerks up. "If you were killed then, why are you wearing jeans? Why aren't you wearing the clothes you wore when you died? Did they even have jeans back then?"

I take a deep breath. "I wasn't wearing anything when I died." I was tied up in rope, but that hardly counts as clothing.

Ashley puts her hand to her mouth. "Sorry," she says contritely. I can see the curiosity in her eyes.

I wasn't naked *after* I died. I remember walking around the house in my blue dress, the lighter dress, the dress I should have worn. When I finally was able to think straight I realized that I'd made up the dress, somehow, that I'd managed to clothe myself with my mind. That's why I'm wearing jeans now, that's why I sometimes wore a poodle skirt in the nineteen–fifties. That's why I'm wearing anything at all. Lizzie probably got the real blue dress after my family realized I wasn't coming home. I hope wearing it didn't make her too sad.

I rub my fingers across the nubbiness of the cushion. I can feel the rough texture under my skin, but I make no indentation in the cushion itself.

"So," I begin, then my voice seems to disappear. I bite my lip and blink a few times, focusing on my fingers as they move back and forth across the fabric. I want to explain about the clothes, but I keep picturing Lizzie in my dress. My chest aches so. If only I could see Lizzie again!

"I'm really sorry. You don't have to talk about it, okay?" Ashley reaches her hand out to touch me, then draws it back. "What will happen if I touch you? Will it be like when you touched Savannah?"

I stop rubbing the couch and look up. "I don't rightly know." I eye Ashley's still-outstretched hand as if it were a large, hairy spider. "Touching living people is horrible. But if you're alive it's fine. So maybe touching another ghost would be okay?" I keep an eye on her hand. I don't seem to have convinced myself.

"Want to try?"

Not only am I not used to talking with anyone, I'm not used to talking with anyone this energetic. I pull my hair back behind my head and twist it as though I were going to put it up in a bun, hold it there for a moment, then release it.

"I suppose we could." I rest my right hand on the couch next to my leg. I grimace, then move my hand a little closer to Ashley. "Put your hand on mine, but only for a second. Just in case."

What if I enter Ashley's mind and am able to read memories that Ashley can't recall — memories of dying? Experiencing one death was certainly enough!

Ashley reaches her hand towards mine, the movement slow and jerky. I screw my eyes shut. What if she reads *my* memories? What if she finds out all the details of *my* death? My eyes fly open right as Ashley taps me lightly with a finger. I yank my hand back as if her finger were a hot coal.

"Are you okay? I'm sorry, I was just curious — did I hurt you?" Ashley bites her lip.

I stare at my hand, turning it from side to side. It looks just like it always has. Her finger had felt like another person's finger. Warm and soft and *real*.

"Emma, I am *so* sorry. I didn't mean to hurt you."

I poke my hand with my own finger. It feels exactly the same as when Ashley tapped me. "Don't worry," I say absently. I didn't read her mind — it was like being touched by someone else back when I was alive. "It — it didn't hurt." I grin. "It felt — it felt normal."

Ashley lets her breath out in a tremendous sigh. "I thought I'd hurt you. When you did whatever it was you did with Savannah it looked like it was horrible. Like maybe it hurt or something."

I poke my hand a few times, then hold it out to Ashley. "It was horrible. It always is," I say matter-of-factly. I'm too involved in this newfound game to care about the unpleasantness of touching the living. "Here, touch me again!"

Ashley rests her fingers on mine. The slight weight pressing into my knuckles pushes my fingers down — just a bit, but until this, nothing that I've touched since being dead has made any physical impact on me. Other than that stupid wall that I can't pass through, of course.

I laugh, a real, honest-to-God laugh. It's been a long time since I've laughed about something other than a movie.

"I have to be so, *so* careful not to ever come into contact with people." I grab Ashley's hand with both of mine and squeeze it tight. Ghost or no, her skin feels warm against mine. The feeling is wonderful, like drinking a pitcher of cold water from the well after walking for miles in the baking summer heat. I realize I'm clasping her hand as if I am never going to let it go. And I don't want to let it go.

"It's ..." my voice breaks, and I release her hand, deliberately lifting each unwilling muscle. There's a lingering warmth where her skin had been pressed against mine. "It's awfully nice to — to *touch* someone after all of these years."

I can feel tears welling up in my eyes, and I swallow around the lump that has suddenly materialized in my throat. I resist the urge to grab her hand again.

"Um, I'm glad," Ashley replies. She must think I'm plumb crazy. There's no way she can know what it's like to be alone the way that I've been for so long. No matter how many people I've seen over the years, no matter how close I felt to the people who lived in this house or the people who worked in it when it became a store, I've been alone.

I hope she never has to find out what it's like.

"But —" she says, wrinkling her nose. "If we're ghosts, and can move through things, shouldn't we be able to move through each other?"

I blink. It's never occurred to me to think about how I would interact physically with another ghost. Since I've never seen one until Ashley, there wasn't much point in any pondering. I can move through walls and furniture, except for the nonexistent walls of the old house, but I only do that when I want to. Otherwise everything feels solid to me. I can't interact with things the way the living do, so when I sit on the sofa the cushion doesn't sink down under my weight, but I can feel the sofa, and I can feel the fabric of the cushion. It doesn't really make any sense, I suppose, but that's the way it is. That's the way it's always been.

"I don't know what would happen. I've never met any other ghosts." What if I chose to move through Ashley? What if at the same time she was choosing to be solid to me? Would I be able to see her insides? The thought makes me feel all-overish.

"Like, what if you were a ghost and there was another ghost who was mean — if you were always solid to each other, the bad ghost could do bad things to you." She eyes me. "Not that I think you're a bad ghost," she adds quickly.

"Well, let's try and see." I stretch my arm out toward Ashley, my earlier fear gone. Becoming intangible with physical objects is simple, just a matter of thinking differently, that's all. I touch Ashley's shoulder with my hand, then concentrate and reach *through* Ashley. Ashley watches in alarm as my hand disappears inside her shoulder.

"Stop! That's creeping me out!" she yells.

I withdraw my hand and inspect it. I didn't feel her at all that time, but I had absolutely felt her when our hands touched.

"I'm not curious any more," she says firmly. "I think I've learned enough about being a ghost for today!"

"That was so odd," I murmur. "I could see you but not myself, just like going through a wall. But why were you visible and I wasn't?"

Ashley fidgets, pulling her legs underneath her. "Probably because *you* were trying to go through *me*." She crosses her arms. "I am completely freaked out now. Can we talk about something else for a while? No more ghost experiments? Please?"

"Of course," I reply. I refrain from pointing out that this was all her idea. "Well ..."

What should we talk about? What did I used to talk about with my girlfriends or with Lizzie? It's been so long since I actually had a conversation with anyone that I feel stymied.

"Maybe, I mean, if it's okay," Ashley looks contrite. "I'm really curious about how you died, since you know and —" She pauses and makes a face. "And I don't know how *I* died."

I take a deep breath. There is nothing wrong with describing my death to Ashley. It all happened so long ago — and after dying there isn't anything to fear, because nothing can hurt me anymore. But I'm afraid to tell Ashley, afraid to talk about it. Afraid to remember — even though I *do* remember. It's as clear as if it had happened yesterday.

"I'm sorry," Ashley says. "I don't mean to be rude."

She looks like a little rabbit crouched on the sofa, scared to find out what happened to her, trying to distract herself until she knows. Will hearing about my death make it easier to accept her own?

"No, it's okay." I clear my throat, which has gotten knotted up.

We sit there for a moment, the ever-present drone of the television the only sound. Ashley glances up at the screen, then back at me. I pull my legs up next to my chest and hug them. He can't hurt me any more. He must have died long ago himself. Then why is this so hard?

"I was — I was picking flowers for my mother, out by the little creek." My fingers are white, they're gripping my legs so tightly. I don't want to talk about this! I should think of Ashley, not me — this might help her, it might make her own death less frightening. Maybe.

My eyes flit from side to side, then focus on Ashley.

I would tell Lizzie if I thought it would help her.

"A creek near here?" Ashley prompts.

I run my hand through my hair.

"Yes, the creek south of town. It's the only one nearby, I'm sure you know of it."

"There's no creek around here." Ashley stares up at the ceiling and thinks for a moment. "Wait, there's a little bridge through Settlers' Park, but that's not south of town. The city goes on for a long while past that. Me and Scott used to play in that park when we lived on Norman Street."

"I suppose that could be it."

How big is the town now? I knew things had changed since I was alive, but I guess I didn't realize how much. Back when I was alive the creek was miles from here, and the town was a mere cluster of buildings compared to the city of Boulder, nestled in the foothills over to the west.

"They have maps up front, I'll go grab one." Ashley starts to rise. "Oh, crap. I guess I can't pick it up."

She sits back down and scowls. I know exactly how she feels. It's hard to see things all around you, but never, ever be able to *do* anything with them. At one point there was talk of turning this place into a bookstore instead of a video store, and I can only imagine how frustrating that would have been — looking at book jackets, reading snippets of stories over people's shoulders, but never being able to read a whole book.

"There was a boulder near it, downstream," I continue. "A huge chunk of rock, as big as a wagon."

It must have been carried there by the glaciers that covered the land years ago. Lizzie and I called the boulder Wagon Rock because when we were little we would scramble up it and pretend we were settlers heading out west in a covered wagon again, like when we were little and we moved out to the Colorado Territory.

"Oh, right!" Ashley exclaims. "I know where that is! It's gray with big white streaks."

I smile. "Yes, that's the one. It's odd to think that the places I used to go are places that you know."

Did Ashley and her brother climb up the same rock when they were younger? I wriggle my fingers, remembering the rough feel of stone as I climbed up the boulder.

"So — that day I was picking flowers."

~~~~~

It was a bright, sunny day in late May, the air crisp and clear, the sunshine warm in the morning, a reminder of the heat it would soon bring in the summertime. Wildflowers were scattered through the field; there was ragwort and flax and the little purple flowers that were Mama's favorite. A light breeze rustled the leaves of the cottonwoods, and the creek churned noisily away, the water running fast and cold, bringing with it the chill of the mountains where it had recently rested as snow. I set down the basket I'd been filling with blossoms. Normally Lizzie and I gathered flowers together, but today she was playing dolls with her friend Nellie.

I smiled. I didn't need dolls anymore — I was a woman, not a girl. I had just turned nineteen, and had my first kiss last night. The whole world seemed different now. I ran a finger lightly over my lips, remembering the warmth I'd felt inside when Ned had held me, how his big, strong arms had engulfed mine. Such a far cry from the dirty little boy who used to pull my pigtails!

I plucked a single yellow flower and twirled the stem in my fingers so the petals whirled around like a kaleidoscope, the buttery gold center glowing like a miniature sun.

"Afternoon, Miss."

A deep, husky voice interrupted my musings. I dropped the flower and turned around. A man stood by the creek, his clothes threadbare and dirty, his scraggly beard in desperate need of a trim. He clasped a worn, grey hat that he began to twist and wring.

"Afternoon," I replied. I didn't recognize the man — no, wait, I had seen him before. But where?

He stared at me, his eyes light and cold. A chill ran down my back in spite of the warmth of the sunshine. The prairie was my home; I'd been running free around here since we'd moved to this part of Colorado when I was barely five. But there were more people here now, and some of them were a bit rough — especially the men from the mining towns — and this man looked like he'd come from the mountains. Was that why he seemed familiar? Had I seen him in town, at the bank, or maybe loitering outside the saloon?

I started to move toward my basket, but he stepped over to it first, his strides long and fast. He plucked it up off the grass and thrust it toward me. Some of the flowers spilled out and fell in a colorful tangle to the ground.

"Thank you," I said, taking the handle, but he didn't let go.

We stood there for a moment, holding the basket between us, his pale eyes fixed on mine, drilling into my soul.

"I'd best be going home now." I tugged at the basket, but he didn't release his grasp. A trickle of sweat ran down my neck.

"You're a lovely young woman." He smiled, revealing a few missing teeth. "You married?"

My heart thumped. I had to get back home, I should turn and run!

"No sir." I swallowed. "But — but I have a fellow."

Thinking of Ned made me feel stronger. I eyed the stranger, trying to think of the fastest way back to where there'd be someone else around. Home was a mile or two away, but Nate Solomon's place was closer. Should I run now? It wasn't right to be rude to people, and running away certainly was rude — but all my instincts were screaming that this man was dangerous. I tensed my body, trying to judge when to start moving.

"A young woman like yourself, not married? All nubile and pristine?" He laughed, a scratchy, deep laugh that made me want to clap my hands over my ears.

I let go of the basket, grabbed my skirts, and ran like the wind.

"Where the hell are you going?" he yelled. "Bitch!"

I glanced back — he was chasing me, swearing up a storm the whole time. I hoped I was faster than he was. The sun was hot on my back, and my skirts were heavy in my arms. Darn my dress! I should have worn the blue one, which was a light cotton, but the air in the morning had been cool, so I'd put on warmer clothing.

I could hear him close behind me, his breathing heavy. I was almost at the Solomon place — I could see Nate and one of his sons out front of the house working on a plow. They could hear me if I screamed, but I didn't have breath enough to both scream and run. I'd be there in a minute, and if they would only turn they would see me!

My left foot landed on a rock and I gasped as I flew forward, plummeting face down into the ground, landing so hard all the wind was knocked clear out of me. The man was right behind, closer than I'd thought, and he landed on top of me, his breath hot on my shoulder, his heavy body weighing me down. I twisted and squirmed, trying to keep him from pinning my arms, and opened my mouth to scream. He punched my face, hard, and my head jerked back.

Why didn't they turn around? Why didn't they see me?

He grabbed a rock and swung it down, down toward my head; I tried to roll away but he had me held good and tight.

And then there was nothing.

~~~~~

"Wow, that sounds like something from a movie!" Ashley's eyes are as round as saucers. "So that's how you died?"

"No." I feel as if I'd just attempted that mad dash all over again. I remember seeing Nate and his son standing there, so close. So close! But they were facing the wrong way, and I was too far away for them to hear anything. Why had I gone so far away to find flowers? There had been plenty in the fields nearer to home.

"He took me back to his house."

I've tried not to think about all of this for years, and telling Ashley is like living it all again. I stare up at the ceiling, absently noting the slight indentation Jimmy Peterson made in the plaster when he was trying to learn how to juggle. Starting with baseballs hadn't been the best choice — his mother had never found out how her favorite vase had really been broken.

"It wasn't exactly his house. There was a farm south of town that used to belong to an English family, but they only lived there for a few years before heading back east. So there was no one living there at the time, and that's where he took me and — and kept me there for a while, and —" My voice quavers, and I take a deep breath.

"And then he killed me."

Time in the house had passed slowly. It had only been a week or so, but it had felt like months. He'd dragged me across the fields and left me on the wooden floor, right over by where the old front door used to be. That's where I came to, trussed up like a cow at a roundup. And then —

"I don't want to talk about this anymore," I declare firmly, and stand up. I can feel Ashley's eyes on me. I said I'd tell her how I died, but I don't have to tell her right now. Or ever! I don't!

I walk over to the nearest case of movies, rest my hand on the top shelf, and notice the first title; *Catch Me If You Can.* He caught me, all right.

I promised to tell Ashley what happened — but I don't have to tell her everything. I don't ever have to tell anyone everything.

"When he finally killed me he, um," I clear my throat. "He strangled me with a piece of rope."

I'd *wanted* to die, I'd wanted the pain to stop, and I'd felt guilty for welcoming what I knew was escape. Could my welcoming the end of my life be why I was trapped here? Did I imprison myself in my ghostly state by being happy to die? I clear my throat. Maybe I did, maybe I didn't. But I am here now, and feeling guilty about something that happened more than a hundred years ago would gain me nothing. But —

If only I'd run faster that day! If only Nate and his son had seen me! If only I'd been able to untie myself!

If only.

I face Ashley, who is still on the sofa, frozen in the same position as when I started my story. Her eyes are fixed on me, her hands clasped tightly in her lap. I force a smile, a short, quick smile, my lips thin and tight. I know it looks fake, but I have to try to reassure Ashley, just like I would Lizzie. I have to be strong. Soon she'll find out what happened to her, and I want to help her. As much as I can.

"It's okay, really. It's —"

I glance up at the ceiling again, and think of Jimmy. He was so much fun to watch grow up. He's my favorite out of all the children who lived in this house, maybe because he reminded me so much of Freddie when he was little. Yet even Jimmy is dead now.

But Ashley is here.

"It's difficult for me to talk about this." I sit back down on the sofa, resting my elbow on the back of the couch and propping up my head with my hand. "But it's awfully good to have someone to tell it to."

As I speak the words a warmth spreads through my body. It really does feel good to have told her. I feel as though I had been carrying around a heavy weight that has suddenly lightened.

"I'm so sorry, so very sorry," Ashley murmurs. "That sounds so awful!"

We sit there for a moment, then Ashley rubs her eyes with her knuckles, scrunching up her face as if she just ate something sour. She looks at me and opens her mouth, then closes it and stares at the arm of the sofa.

"I wonder —" She puts a hand to her lips, then clasps her hands neatly in her lap and wriggles her feet. She takes a deep breath and holds it for a moment.

"I wonder what happened to me."

Four

We sit next to one another for some time, each lost in our own thoughts. I'm worn out from remembering. I can still recall every detail perfectly. Every bruise, every scrape, every broken bone. Talking with Ashley made me feel better, much to my surprise, but those memories have been etched inside of me, forever.

I stare at the dingy charcoal carpeting that covers the pine floorboards. The carpet is so thin in places that I wonder if the fabric will eventually wear away completely and reveal the wood underneath.

So much has happened in this house, so many people have lived here — three families, seven children. Along with eight dogs, six cats, three rabbits, many, many gerbils, and a very loud, poorly mannered parrot. I've watched so much, watched but never participated. It's like I'm inside my very own movie. Except that I'm standing just offstage in every scene.

The front door locks with its familiar click, and I hear a giggle from the counter area. It must be around ten o'clock. Stacia and Vicki will clean up, then leave in another fifteen minutes or so. What was Matt doing here earlier? I sigh and close my eyes, imagining what it would have been like if Matt, not Ashley, had shown up here as a ghost.

A loud series of thumps, followed by the inevitable creak on the loose step, tells me Vicki has just come down from upstairs. Ashley perks up.

"What's going on?"

I open my eyes and watch her clamber up onto the arm of the sofa, her head craned toward the back of the store. As obsessed as I am with my fantasies about Matt, he can't compete with Ashley for my attention. She can *see* me, she can *hear* me. I feel a warmth inside, a happiness I haven't felt since I was alive. I have a friend.

"Closing time."

At least I have a friend while she's here. But what if Ashley decides to leave? I wouldn't be able to follow her — I'd be left alone. The joy I felt a moment ago has been replaced by a tightness in my belly.

"Oh, right." She stands up on the cushion, her feet resting precariously on the arm and the back of the old sofa, and peers over the top of the nearest rack of DVDs. "Now what?"

I put my hand up to pull her back down before she falls, then remember she's dead. Nothing bad would happen if she fell. I jerk back and clasp my hands together in my lap before she notices.

"What do you mean? They'll close the store, then go home." Is she expecting a parade of elephants? What does she think is going to happen?

"What happens at night? I don't feel at all sleepy. And where do we sleep anyway? Or do we disappear at night?"

"Disappear?"

"Well, yeah!" She turns toward me and almost loses her balance, apparently excited by the notion. "Surely we still sleep. Or something. Don't we?"

I shake my head. "No. At least I don't sleep." My eyes narrow. "Although I suppose *you* might." That would just figure.

"No way!" She moves a foot slightly and puts a hand on the wall to catch herself. She'd better not be able to sleep when I can't. To sleep again, to dream …

I grit my teeth and think about how easily I could push her off onto the floor. It's not as though it would hurt her.

She flops down next to me and watches as Stacia walks down the aisle carrying a small stack of movie cases. "So what *do* we do?"

"Do?" We … haunt? Hope? Cry?

She stares at me as if I'm an imbecile. "What do we do during the night? Does anything happen? Do we go somewhere else?"

I wish I'd pushed her off the couch.

"I usually stand by the window and watch the street outside. I watch the people and cars go by. Or I, uh, look at the sky."

This sounds ridiculously sad and pathetic when I say it out loud. And it is. But there isn't much else I can do, stuck in this place. As boring as my days of people-watching often are, there's even less to watch at night. Especially at this time of year. The days are shorter and colder, and fewer people are out late.

Ashley already has a funny expression on her face. I can only imagine how much more wretched she'll think I am if I tell her how desperately I look forward to springtime every year. I clear my throat, continuing to impress Ashley with my dull, horrible life.

"Then after a while I'll sit on the sofa and make up stories for myself. Until morning, when there are people on the streets to watch, and then, of course, the store opens."

I refrain from mentioning that I traverse the boundaries of the old house at least once a night, usually more, or that I occasionally entertain myself by counting the number of movies on each shelf, or by trying to memorize all the movie titles in a category.

"Wow." She rests her chin on her fist, her head nodding slightly, as if she's agreeing with herself about something. "That sounds — Well, no offense, but that sounds incredibly boring. Why don't you go somewhere else? Why do you hang out here anyway?"

"I can't go anywhere else," I mutter. This isn't how I *want* to spend my nights — or my days, for that matter.

"Sure you can! Just 'cause you have to haunt this place doesn't mean you have to stay here all the time!"

She doesn't understand. There's no way she could understand. But her simplification of my life is awfully grating. Especially since *she* isn't stuck here.

Stacia edges closer to us, her perfectly manicured nails bright in the harsh light. I'm irritated with Stacia for infringing on our space, but it's not her fault. It's not like she can *see* us. And I know I'm really not angry with her, I'm angry with Ashley. I shouldn't be mad at her either, but it's hard not to direct my anger at her since she is the only person here. The only one I can interact with, at least. And *she* can leave the store. *She* isn't tied to this stupid building for all eternity!

I glare at Stacia. She doesn't have any idea how lucky she is. If *I* were alive today I wouldn't be squandering my time working in a video store. I'd go to college and learn all sorts of interesting things. In my time it was absolutely impossible for me to go to college. Even if my family had been able to afford it, I'm a girl, and back then girls hardly ever got to do anything other than get married. These days anyone can go to college. That's what I would do. I'd be a doctor or a lawyer or a secret agent, just like in all those movies. And I would be married too, with lots of children. I would have married Ned, if I could have. But I'd *do* something too. If I wasn't dead.

"I'm stuck here. I can't leave," I snarl. "I try every day."

Every single day.

"What?" Ashley wrinkles her forehead. "That doesn't make any sense."

"Obviously not." My voice snaps like the crack of a whip. "The house I was killed in burned down — this is the second house. I can't leave the walls of the first house, even though they don't even exist anymore."

Ashley stares at me, then blinks.

"Wow. That totally sucks!"

I take a deep breath; it isn't Ashley's fault, it isn't Stacia's fault. For all I know it is *my* fault I'm tied to the stupid, invisible, nonexistent house.

"Yes, it su —" I stop, finding it hard to use a word so foreign to my time in spite of the fact that I hear it spoken all the time. "Yes it does."

Ashley's expression is filled with sympathy, or perhaps pity. Whatever it is, it makes me even more annoyed, so I cross my arms and watch Stacia as she files each movie case back in order, making sure every row of cases is neatly straightened. People today spend so much of their time on tawdry pursuits, like movies and television and video games and shopping. When I was alive, we certainly didn't spend all our time on chores, but no one squandered time like this. Don't they realize how lucky they are to have the time?

I smile, knowing my memories are rose-colored. We didn't have the sheer amount of time to spend on movies and such that people have in today's world. There was always something to do, and it was usually important — sewing, cooking, washing clothes, taking care of the animals. If we'd had more time we probably would have happily 'squandered' it.

Stacia reaches our end of the row and rests her hand on the shelf next to Ashley. I'm lost in my thoughts, so it takes me a second to realize she's just put her hand *through* Ashley. Ashley doesn't seem to be aware of what is happening; she is still looking at me with that irritating, compassionate expression. Stacia is so close I can smell the perfume she always wears; there's a faint scent of lilacs that always reminds me of our last visit to Grandma's before we made the long trek out to

Colorado. I catch my breath, knowing it's too late to warn Ashley to get out of the way — but she doesn't seem bothered in the least. Doesn't she feel Stacia's mind? How can Ashley not notice *that*?

"What?" Ashley asks.

I point, unable to say anything. Ashley's eyes follow my finger, and she finally realizes Stacia is there just as the woman pulls her hand out of Ashley's torso. Ashley leaps back, away from Stacia.

"Hey, that's creepy!" She looks at Stacia as if the other woman was a soiled rag. "Did you see that? Her arm was inside of me!"

Creepy? If someone touches me, my being becomes entwined with theirs in a way that is as awful as the sound of nails on a chalkboard to my very *soul*, and to Ashley that's merely 'creepy'?

"What's up, Emma? I don't get it." She glances at Stacia, then edges closer to me.

"Didn't you feel her?" I pull my knees up to my chest and hug them. My eyes flick back and forth between Stacia and Ashley. If Stacia had touched me I'd have dashed to the other side of the building by now and would be trying desperately to shake the horrible sense of *being someone else* out of my head.

"No, why? Oh!" Her mouth forms a big pink O to match. "Hey, why didn't I? You said it's bad to touch people, right? I didn't even notice!"

"Did you really not feel anything?" I hug my knees tighter. This makes no sense. I saw Stacia's arm go *through* Ashley.

Stacia steps over to the next shelf, oblivious to the consternation she's caused. She's humming something under her breath.

Ashley shakes her head at me. "Nothing. I felt nothing." Her eyes zip back and forth between me and Stacia.

"Wait! I have an idea!" She dashes over next to Stacia, makes a funny grimace, then rams her hand through Stacia's left shoulder. She moves her arm all around — left and right, up and down. The only thing I can see is Ashley's arm heading straight into Stacia's back, then vanishing. My spine prickles.

"I don't feel anything!" She looks at me expectantly. "How come?"

Apparently, since I've been a ghost for a while I'm the expert. I don't feel like one — I'm as perplexed as she is. And I'm right irritated. Not only can Ashley leave the building, and apparently go anywhere she wants, but she also doesn't get zapped like I do whenever she touches a living person.

"I have no idea." I dig my nails into the sides of my legs. Why are things different for her? This isn't exactly fair. Why don't my stupid rules apply to her?

Stacia continues down the aisle. As she moves away Ashley's arm gradually becomes visible again. The scent of lilacs lingers.

Ashley watches her for a moment, then turns back to me.

"Well, that was pretty weird." She twists a lock of hair around a finger. "Hey, are you okay? You look really pissed off."

I am, but I try to look normal. "No, of course not. I'm — I'm just a little, um, frustrated, is all."

Frustrated doesn't even cover it. *Jealous*, maybe. *Livid.* I release my legs and squirm until I'm sitting cross-legged.

"Frustrated? What do you mean?"

I scratch an imaginary itch on my arm. I haven't been itchy since I was alive.

"I spend a lot of my time avoiding people — living people." I rub my palms on my knees. "I don't understand why when *you* touch someone you don't feel anything. And it doesn't make sense that you can leave this … this place, but I can't."

It's not her fault. There has to be an explanation. Doesn't there?

"Oh, I get it." She nods. "Yeah, you're pretty much getting screwed, aren't you?"

I want to smack her. "Look, I've been here for over a hundred years and I'm used to my restrictions, but it's a little difficult to have you show up and be able to do things that I can't."

She'll probably be able to fall asleep, too — it certainly wouldn't surprise me at this point.

"I'm sorry." Her eyes flicker about, as if she is afraid to meet mine. "I don't know why things are different for me. I don't think it's very fair either. But — but you're the only person in the world who can see me, and I'd really like to be friends. Please don't be mad."

She clasps her hands together, the one holding the other so tightly that the bones of her knuckles show clearly through the whitened skin. I clench my jaw and can feel my teeth grind together.

"I'm not mad at you; I'm not. It's just … it's just hard to be stuck here. I'm —"

I catch myself before I say anything else. My skin feels as if it's buzzing with electricity, and I want to run or jump or scream — I can barely keep myself still. I *want* to tell her that I'm tired of having all these dumb rules. I'm tired of being alone all the time, of being invisible to every person, bird, and insect I see. I'm tired of never being able to sleep, of never having any break from the sameness of my existence. I'm tired of wandering around and around these stupid racks of movies, of having to be on alert whenever there are living people in the store so that I don't get touched by them. Of having to watch people talk to each other while I stand there unnoticed, like a piece of furniture or a wall. I'm tired of being afraid all by myself when it's dark and I can't stop remembering my murder. I'm tired of being unable to leave this horrible, boring, stupid prison.

I'm tired of being alone.

But I don't say any of this. If Ashley thinks I'm too pathetic, too desperate, she might leave.

Because she can. Even if I can't.

The silence of the store fills my ears.

"I want to be friends too," I whisper. Even if Ashley turns out to be a horrible person, I can't not want her to be my friend. How could I? She can see me, she can hear me.

She makes me feel *real.*

Ashley does a little bounce. "Oh, I'm glad!" She grins at me, and I smile back. Apparently we're friends again.

"Why is touching someone so awful?" She peers down the aisle in the direction Stacia went. "Reading somebody else's mind sounds pretty cool to me."

I don't know how to respond. I don't know how to tell her what it's like to be in another person's mind, to be you and someone else at the same time. I take a deep breath.

"When I touch other people I sort of, well, become them." That doesn't sound clear at all.

"How can you be someone else? You're still Emma."

"I don't know how to explain it. I'm me, and I'm the other person." Is there an analogy that might make sense to her? "Think of wearing someone else's clothes as being like wearing someone else's thoughts." This isn't a great comparison, but it will have to do. "Imagine that you're you, Ashley, then suddenly you're wearing clothes that don't fit right. Not only do you not like them, but they're also uncomfortable. You're still you, but you don't feel like yourself."

She rubs a finger across her lips. "I think I see what you mean. So when you touch another person you're wearing their thoughts, their opinions."

Maybe it was a good analogy after all. "I suppose you could think of it like that." Although when you take off your clothing, the memory of wearing it — the texture of the fabric, where something rubbed too much against your skin, the tightness or looseness in different areas — that doesn't linger the way someone else's memories, their loves and hates, their emotions, their *presence*, sticks after I'm in their mind.

"Isn't it fun sometimes? "

"No! It's never fun. It's horrible!" I snap. She jumps slightly, surprised by my vehemence. What is she thinking? How could having your identity submerged by another be fun? I close my eyes for a second and try to calm myself down.

"Think of it as being thousands and thousands of times worse than wearing someone else's clothes."

"I get that part." She nods, as if she really does get it. Which she clearly does *not*. "But ..." She raises her eyebrows. "Isn't it kind of neat — after you're done, when you're out of them, I mean, and it's all over — to be able to read someone else's mind?"

Neat?

"No. It isn't." It is never "neat", never fun. What is she talking about?

"I learn things, I guess," I say after a moment. I tug at the hem of my shirt, then start twisting it around my fingers.

"When I touch someone I read that person's thoughts. I feel what they feel." Whether I want to or not. "And sometimes I learn something new. Like what it feels like to ride in an automobile, or to eat avocados."

Everything is different, depending on who I touch. Avocados might taste one way to one person, but another to someone else. It's interesting in a way, I suppose, but I've never learned anything that I couldn't do without.

And I've never touched a person and not felt myself squelched.

Sometimes, especially when it goes on for a long time, I get frightened that I won't be able to become *me* again.

"Honest, Ashley, the whole thing is so awful it's not worth anything I might learn."

Ashley looks fascinated "That is so cool!" she exclaims. "I wish I could do it!"

Clearly I haven't explained myself well.

I blink as the lights go out.

"Oh!" Ashley squeals, and claps her hands together. I can see her just fine. Part of being a ghost, for me at least, is being able to see remarkably well in the dark. It's one of the few positives. "Hey, I can see!"

Apparently she has the same ability — she seems to have gotten all the good ghost characteristics, but none of the bad.

"That's great." My voice sounds a little flat.

Ashley tromps around the store, inordinately elated at being able to see in the dark. I suppose discovering ghostly vision could be exciting, at first. None of my new abilities were all that fun for me to discover because I was so alone, so frightened, so desperate to escape the house — just like I'd wanted to escape it when I was alive. Having recently been murdered detracted somewhat from the excitement of finding I could move through things or the realization I was able to see in the dark. I figured out a lot of my ghostly qualities early on — night vision, the boundaries, of course, and touching people.

At the beginning the only person around to touch was *him*, and I didn't mean to do it. It happened right after my death — I'd been dead a minute, maybe two. I was standing there, staring at my still warm body, and he stepped into me. He was thinking about me, and — naturally — his thoughts were atrocious. So much glee at having killed me, and what he wanted to do with my corpse … I had no idea a human being could even contemplate such actions. Maybe I have such a difficult time touching people because he was the first person I ever touched.

I shake my head, trying to banish my memories.

"Hey, Emma!" Ashley's voice is distant — she must be on the far side of the store. "Do you — I mean, did you, I guess. Did you have any brothers and sisters?"

"Yes," I respond. "A brother and a sister."

I can hear a soft rustle to my right. It's getting closer — she's walking back toward me. I glance toward the front of the store. I can't see through the window from my seat on the couch, but the light from the street outside reflects off the ceiling, growing brighter and then dimming as a car drives by. I lean my head on the back of the sofa and stare at the ceiling, which has become a light gray color to my ghostly night eyes.

"Do you?" Oh right, I remember her saying something about her brother and a car, but I can't recall his name. "Besides your brother, that is. What's his name again?" I wait a minute, then decide she must not have heard me.

"Ashley, what is your brother's name?"

She's right around the corner — I heard her there a second ago — but she doesn't reply. Fine. She can be difficult if she wants. I'll just stop talking to her too. I cross my arms and glare in her direction.

After a moment I feel bad. I know my irritation is at my situation, not at her. I'm the older, wiser ghost, just as when I was alive I was the older, wiser sister. I should just tell her this kind of joke isn't funny. She can't know how similar it is to my past hundred plus years of solitude.

"Ashley?" I get up and go look down the aisle she was in when I last heard her voice. The two shelves of movies stretch away, unconcerned with the emptiness of the space between them.

"Ashley? Where are you?"

Shadows race from one side of the ceiling to the other as another car drives by. I feel skittish, unnerved. Ashley must be playing a game, although it's a pretty stupid game. I used to play hide and seek with Lizzie and Freddie, but there isn't much point in playing unless the other person knows about it.

I trudge back to the sofa and sit down, rubbing the goose bumps on my arms. She'll get bored soon enough — and then she can apologize.

I sulk for a while in the silence of the store before admitting to myself that she might not be playing a game after all. She must have gotten angry and left, although for the life of me I can't think what I could have possibly done to offend her. I hug my legs to my chest and press my face against them. None of this makes any sense. Ashley doesn't seem like the kind of person who would get upset and run off without a word.

I raise my head and rest my chin on my knees. When she left earlier she remembered leaving, but not returning. What if something *made* her leave? My mind runs through all of the ghost movies I've seen over the years, but nothing matches. Besides, ghosts aren't usually the ones in danger in the movies. Usually they're evil, or else they're like me — stuck. But what if there's another ghost that is taking Ashley away? Or what if it's something else, like an alien?

I shiver and squeeze my legs so tight they hurt. I scan the room but everything looks as it always does. Everything I can see, that is. I'm afraid to move, afraid whatever it is will come and take me away too.

But what if Ashley needs my help? It seems unlikely that I'd be able to do anything to save her from anything alien or an evil ghost, but I have to look for her. Which is easier said than done right now.

I swallow and try to convince myself to move out of my frozen little ball. It takes a few minutes before I'm able to put my feet back on the floor. My movements are slow and deliberate, like a cat trying to sneak by a sleeping dog. I peer around the nearest shelf, but there's no one there — no Ashley, no aliens, no evil ghosts. Nothing. The same with the next aisle.

I move across the room, my motions quickening. This is ridiculous. I've been haunting here for *years*. Something odd is going on, but there's a reason. I'm not in a movie. Whatever happened is *real*. I move faster and faster, my eyes searching the gloom. "Ashley?" I hear myself call. I'm afraid — afraid to be caught by whatever caught her, afraid for her, afraid I'm too late and she's gone forever. "Ashley!" My pace has quickened so much that I'm running. I dash from room to room, sprinting up the stairs and flinging myself through the walls and shelves with an abandon I would never allow myself during the day when I might run into a living person. "Ashley!" I run and I search and I run and I search, and I can't find her. She isn't here. I'm alone and she's gone, and I don't want her to be gone, and I want her to be okay, and something happened to her, and it's like right after I died when I finally realized that I was *dead* and trapped, and I ran around and around the house, my prison, running into the walls and beating at them and I was alone and scared and trapped and dead and alone —

I stop at the bottom of the stairs, my imaginary heart pounding away like mad. She's gone. I don't know how or why or where, but she's gone. I slide down until I'm sitting on the bottom step. A lock of hair falls in front of my face, and as I brush it away I realize my face is wet. I didn't even realize I'd been crying. I wipe my eyes on my sleeve and take a deep breath.

She's really gone.

And I was a fool to panic. There are no aliens, no monsters. Ashley just plumb ran off. Maybe she got angry at me. Or more likely, maybe she remembered something about her death and went off to be alone. I take a deep breath. *That* I can understand, for certain. She came back before, so she'll come back again. Probably.

I square my shoulders. There's nothing I can do to *make* her come back, so I'll just have to wait and see. And hope.

I sit there for some time before deciding to check the boundaries. I can't sit here like a log all night, and in spite of the frustration of reaffirming my imprisonment I've found that walking the boundaries is usually calming. I guess if you do something just about every day for decade after decade you get accustomed to it, even if you're dead.

I sigh and use the banister to pull myself up. I so hope Ashley comes back. I like having her around. I like having someone to talk to. I like that she can see me.

I stand there for a moment, my hand resting on the smooth wood rail.

I like not being alone.

I follow my regular path and start where the front door of the original house used to be. In this house it is just a spot in the middle of the wall closest to the street. But I know exactly where the door was; two steps from the south wall of today, nine from the south wall of the past.

I run my fingers over the wall in the present, while my mind feels the solidity of the wooden door of the past. I walk down the room, methodically running the palm of my hand along the wall, my arm and hand reaching through the shelves of movies to touch the invisible wall which shares the space of the visible one. I slow when I come to the first window.

I stop to look out through the glass. The beams of the streetlight shine through the window and illuminate a section of the store. I stand there for a moment, pressing my face against the glass, my skin savoring its coolness while my mind feels the rough texture of plaster against my cheek. I look across the street at the florist's shop and the little shops in the converted houses on either side of it, then turn back to my task. My fingers trail along the wall until I reach my boundary. In today's world there is no wall here, just two more aisles of movies. I push against the intangibility of the corner of the old house with my hands. It's there as always, rigidly right-angled in spite of the determined flatness of the visible wall.

I turn to the west and continue my patrol, my hand pressed flat against empty space as I cross the aisle between shelves of movies, feeling the ever-present resistance of the wall that isn't there. I walk through shelves, sticking with my path in spite of the inanimate objects in my way.

I follow my bounding wall past the bathroom, then reach the next invisible corner and turn south, dragging my fingers along the wall as I cross in front of the stairs to the second floor. The door to the basement is on the west side of the middle wall, just where it was in the original house. I walk quickly past it. Even now — well over a century after my murder in the old cellar — I still find it uncomfortable to even think of going downstairs. I make myself check the boundaries there just as I do everywhere else, but it's so difficult that I only go downstairs once every few months, if that. I pause, trying to remember what I did during my ridiculous panic earlier. It's all a bit of a blur, which is probably for the best because I'm none too proud of the way I acted. Aliens, really!

The unseen wall is rough under my fingertips as my hand scrapes across the open air. Suddenly I hear a muffled noise. A sharp sound, like a broom being dropped on a stone floor, but softened, as if I'm hearing it through a thick blanket. I pause, hand still on the nonexistent plaster, and turn my head toward the basement door. No one is down there, no one ever goes down there, but I could swear the noise came from behind the closed and locked door.

I stand there for a moment, waiting for the sound to repeat itself. A motor guns loud outside, the thick reverberations vibrating through the walls, the floor, rattling the DVDs. I keep myself still as a rabbit watching a coyote as the car speeds off into the night and the harsh noise fades away.

No sound came from the basement; no sound *could* have come from the basement. I must have heard something from outside, and my persistent, irrational fear of the underneath of this house — of the old house — had fed on the noise. I've made a sure enough fool of myself tonight already; I don't need to add even more silliness.

I take a deep breath and walk on, trailing my fingers on the wall that isn't there.

Five

I finish tracing the boundaries, then stand by the second floor window in the little bedroom which now houses Independent films — fitting, considering that this used to be Jimmy Peterson's room. I used to lurk in this same corner watching Jimmy play with the collection of odds and ends he kept in an old shoebox — little boy treasures like rocks and marbles and an old flint arrowhead he'd found.

I lean against the window frame and watch the empty street, entertaining myself with my memories. They're my escape, my drug — they're familiar and safe and easy. Worrying about whether or not Ashley will come back is not.

I try to immerse myself in my reminiscences, but my mind keeps spinning back to Ashley. Over the years I've taught myself to pretend, to push my worries aside, because there's nothing I can do to change the reality of my situation.

But I can't distract myself from hoping that Ashley will come back.

After a while I admit that I can't think of anything else. I trudge down the stairs, my steps slow. Having Ashley around was like the warm, happy feeling I remember when I'd feel the sunshine on my face after being cooped up inside during a long storm, and now it's as if the clouds have descended once again.

My hand slides along the carved banister, and I survey the store as I descend. The counter is empty, a faint glow coming from one of the computers on the desk behind it. The employees sit where the kitchen used to be. Mrs. Briarwood, the woman who owns the store, had the wall ripped out and installed a countertop instead, with posts going all the way to the ceiling on either side of it.

I scan the aisles of DVDs in the main room. The light from the streetlamp brightens the southern side of the building, causing the shelves to cast long, dark shadows that stretch out across the carpeted floor. The street outside is quiet. I turn back to the counter and pause, my hand gripping the railing, my left foot frozen with my toes barely touching the next step.

Ashley is perched on the counter, her back pressed up against a post. One foot rests on the countertop, while her other leg hangs off the edge and dangles in the air. She's staring at the board that lists what movies have just arrived. The glow from the computer's screensaver illuminates her outline, the color shifting from green to blue to red as the unseen image changes.

I swallow. How did she get there so quickly? I'd looked away for a split second, not nearly enough time for her to walk through the building and leap up on the counter.

She doesn't seem to know I'm on the stairs, unless she is pretending to not see me. I hold my breath. That notion makes no sense whatsoever, but neither does her appearing so quickly. Could she be playing a trick on me? But why? I crouch down, hoping that I won't hit a squeaky board — then I chastise myself as I remember that, as a ghost, I wouldn't make any sound if I did.

She turns away from the movie listings and sighs, a long, heavy sigh, as her eyes wander around the store. Her gaze passes over the stairs, but she doesn't see me. Or else she does and is pretending she doesn't. I press my lips together. That would be ridiculous. *I'm* being ridiculous. Ashley is my friend. My friend!

A somewhat enigmatic friend.

She swings her other leg off the counter, grabs the edge of the counter with both hands, and begins twisting her feet in little circles. Her sneakers are such a crisp, bright white that they almost seem to glow in the grayness of our night. She sighs again, so deeply that her exhalation lifts her shoulders and chest, then she purses her mouth, her lips forming a fine, tight line.

Why did Ashley show up here in the first place anyway? She wasn't killed in the store — I would certainly have noticed *that*. Why does she keep coming back here when she is clearly not tied to it like I am? I've been so focused on having a companion that I haven't thought about the fact that she might be here because she needs my help. I close my eyes. How uncharitable of me.

I open my eyes to see an empty countertop.

I sprint down the stairs and dash to the counter, leaning over it to look on the other side. There are several neat stacks of papers, a few shelves containing high-demand films, and the computer, which someone has set to display images from beaches around the world, but no Ashley. The image on the computer screen is of a tiny island of white sand in the midst of the ocean.

"What are you doing?"

At the sound of Ashley's voice I jump as if I've been shocked. I swing around to see her kneeling on the floor in front of the rack of movies across from the counter. The Thriller section, I think bewilderedly. I must have run right past her! Her eyebrows are raised — she probably thinks I'm a lunatic. But her behavior is far more bizarre than mine.

"Where did you come from?" I hear myself squeak, like a little mouse.

"I've been here all night." She stands up and put her hands on her hips. "I was talking with you by the couch," she waves one hand in the direction of where we'd sat earlier. "And then I didn't know where you were, so I've been hanging out here waiting for you." She turns back to the shelf she'd been perusing and resumes looking through the films.

"We should watch a movie — it's pretty boring here at night. I don't know how you put up with it. Have you seen this one?" She points to a case on the shelf.

I ignore whatever it is she's pointing to and stare at her. Boring? She's been dead for two days and is bored already?

"Ashley, you disappeared." She glances at me, her face expressionless, then bends back down next to the shelf of movies. "You asked if I had any brothers and sisters, and then I asked you, and then — you were gone." Doesn't she realize how peculiar this is? How could she go somewhere and not know?

She shrugs. "I don't have any idea what you are talking about. We were telling each other about that stuff, but then you were gone and so I came and sat here, on the counter." Her chin rises slightly. "By *myself*." She emphasizes the last word as if this is all somehow my fault.

Her recollection sounds exactly like mine. Could *I* have disappeared? I think of parallel universes and alternate dimensions, things I only know of from movies. Could they be real after all, and not made-up stories?

"I didn't go anywhere," I insist, my voice firm in spite of my confusion. "You and I were talking about all of that right after the store closed for the night, and now it's hours later."

She runs her hands through her hair and rolls her eyes. "It is *not* later. That was only a few minutes ago. Would you please stop fooling around?"

"Look at the clock." I'm scared to look myself, afraid that maybe I was the one who'd vanished after all.

"Okay, fine," she mutters. "I saw it earlier, but I don't remember where it is." She scuffs the floor with one of her brilliant white sneakers.

"It's above the front door." We both turn toward the clock on the east wall. Its white face shines dimly in the light that trickles in from the front of the store, its black hands strict and firm, implacably declaring the time.

Two thirty–two.

My shoulders relax — I didn't even realize I was tensing them. I didn't disappear, I didn't!

But Ashley most certainly did.

"Hey!" She scrunches up her nose. "How did you do that?"

"Do what?"

"You changed the time on the clock! Everyone knows ghosts can move things if they try really hard." She rolls her eyes. "You live in a video store, hello! Haven't you seen all the movies where ghosts can do stuff like that?"

This is what she's thinking? How dare she act like she knows what I can and can't do?

"Just because something happens in the movies doesn't mean it's true." I snap, and storm back to the sofa, wishing that I could stomp on the floor and make real sounds. I've been haunting here since before her great-great grandparents were born!

Ashley trails behind me. "If you didn't mess with the clock, who did? I remember looking at it just before ten, right around when they closed the store."

Why does she think I told her to look at the darn clock? Why would I show her a clock that didn't display the correct time?

I reach the sofa and fling my body onto the dingy fabric. The cushions remain firm under my nonexistent weight.

"I didn't do anything to the clock, you *disappeared*." I hear myself hiss the last word, which fits my mood. I would like to be a snake right now. I would bite Ashley with my sharp little teeth, then slither off into a hole and hide.

She sits cross-legged on the floor next to me, her eyes reflecting the light from the moon; a soft whitish-yellow beam shines in through the window behind me. The color is soothing, peaceful, not harsh like the light up front from the streetlight.

"How could I disappear?" Her voice sounds normal when she starts her sentence, then lowers, almost to a whisper. "Where could I have gone? Why don't I remember anything?"

"I don't know. You were walking back toward me. I was sitting right here." I pat the sofa. "I asked you if you had any brothers and sisters — and then you weren't there anymore." Her eyebrows have formed two crooked lines, and her eyes are fixed on mine. "I searched all over the store for you, but you were gone." I twirl a finger in my hair. I'm certainly not about to tell her I ran about like a lunatic looking for her, nor that I bawled like a baby because I thought she might have been kidnapped by aliens and that I might be next.

"I don't understand."

"I don't either."

She presses against the edge of the sofa closest to me, and we sit there in silence. She seems to be as confused as I am. I shouldn't have thought she was playing tricks on me. It was scary enough to die and become a ghost. I remember that fear well. But add to that this odd disappearing and reappearing, without even the memory of being gone — it must be truly frightening.

I reach down and pat her shoulder. She's warm, just like a living person would be. Ashley starts at my touch, then smiles. It's a small smile, but a smile nonetheless.

"I'm glad you're here, Emma."

My hand feels warm where it touched her. I wrap my other hand around it and squeeze tight. I'm worried about her.

Something isn't right. I don't know what. And I don't know how to find out.

"I'm glad you're here too."

~~~~~

Ashley and I sit there for a while, her on the floor and me on the sofa, our silence merging with the silence of the empty store. Her expression looks pensive in the moonlight. She could be thinking about her family, or her death, or about all the things she will never be able to do again.

I certainly thought about all of those things when I died. No more staying up late at night, whispering with Lizzie under the covers, telling each other stories while we snuggled together to keep warm. No more tromping through the snow in winter, no splashing barefoot in the creek in the summer. Never again seeing my parents or Lizzie or Freddie. Or Ned. There was no longer any point in thinking about my future, about someday getting married and having children of my own. I had no future. I had no life. It was gone, and all my hopes and dreams were dashed forever. I was dead.

Dying was not like anything I could have ever imagined. I suppose if I ever thought about my death while I was alive I probably imagined that I would live to be an old woman, dying peacefully in my sleep. But, of course, that isn't at all what happened.

One minute I was alive, my breaths short and sharp as I tried to struggle against him, bound as I was, and in pain from beatings so awful I couldn't think straight. My broken wrist throbbed, and as I thrashed about it sent spikes of pain up my arm. I remember crying, pleading, begging him to stop. I'd long since ceased asking him to let me go me. All I wanted was release from the pain.

The rough rope burned as it tightened around my neck, the coarse fibers digging into my skin as they took away my breath, my life. I remember thinking of my family, and of Ned, and of Lizzie in particular.

Then there was nothing, the lack of pain sweet, like Mama rubbing a cool, damp cloth on my head when I was feverish. I felt no sensation at all, not the chill of the cellar floor, not the constriction of the rope around my neck. The dull ache of my many bruises was gone, the piercing of my broken wrist transformed into a blissful numbness.

I must have known I was dead, but it didn't sink in straightaway. I remember standing there, seeing my body lying naked and crumpled on the floor, watching him laugh as he pulled tight on the rope he'd wrapped around my neck. I guess my being dead didn't sink in right away for him either.

When he stepped into me, into me as a ghost, it was as if a hot poker had been rammed into my eye. I became him, for a split second — and though I tried, I couldn't move away. I felt what he felt, thought what he thought, until he walked on and I was no longer trapped in his mind. I don't like to remember what it was like, even now, because it was so awful, so horrid, so foreign to me. How could someone take pleasure in another's pain? How could he be filled with such glee at my agony, full of satisfaction because he'd killed me — and even worse, pleased that it had been so demeaning and painful for me?

Why did he murder *me*?

I sigh.

Ashley rests her hand on my leg, and I start.

"Are you okay?" Her forehead wrinkles as she inspects me, rather like when Mama would worry that I was coming down with a cold. Ashley's brown hair looks silvery gray in this light.

"I'm fine."

I am fine. I've been fine for years. Bored, confused, lonely, frustrated, frightened — but fine.

I rub my eyes. Poor Ashley, entering my world of sleeplessness and intangibility. At least she isn't stuck in this building. Then why am I? I feel a surge of resentment and grit my teeth. There must be some explanation. Maybe she was killed outside somewhere, so she haunts the entire city? Maybe she was killed and cut up into little bits, and one of the bits was brought here? I might not notice a, well, *piece* of a body ... Would that explain her weird disappearances? Maybe she has to go to where each of the pieces are?

Ashley giggles, oblivious to my gory hypothesizing. "Hey, let's rearrange all the DVDs, then watch what happens when the customers come in tomorrow."

She's bounced back awfully quickly.

"We can't move anything. Remember me saying I didn't change the clock? I *can't* change the clock. Neither can you. But we should talk about what's going on with you. Something isn't right." That's an understatement if there ever was one.

"Sure we can! We're ghosts!" She screws up her face and pokes at the arm of the couch with a forefinger. If she were alive she'd be making an indentation in the thick, cushiony fabric, but nothing happens. "Hey! What's the deal? I'm concentrating really hard. That's what you have to do. Right?" She tries pushing on the cushion she's sitting on, with the same lack of effect.

"It just doesn't work." I explain, hoping my smugness isn't showing. At least in this one area she has the same restriction that I do. "All the ghost movies have ghosts who can do things like that, but nothing works for me." I pause. "I do seem to make people cold, although not very cold. But that's it." Of course, I only make people cold when I touch them, and if I touch them I *become* them for a horrible split second, so I don't consider this a very useful skill.

"This sucks!" Ashley crosses her arms and stretches her legs straight out in front of her on the floor. "What other abilities are ghosts supposed to have? I've heard of the cold thing, and the being able to move stuff, like furniture. And making noise — ghosts can make noise." She looks up at me inquisitively.

"I can't make any noise that living people can hear." I've tried everything from singing to whispering to yelling directly into people's ears, and have never gotten a reaction. And in spite of all the tales about animals being able to sense things people can't, none of the pets of any of the families who've lived in this house ever noticed me. Not even that stupid parrot. "But Ashley, we need to talk about *you*."

Ashley frowns and joins me on the couch, then squirms around until she's lying on her back, both legs resting on the wall behind the sofa, her head hanging back off the cushion. It looks surprisingly comfortable, so I wriggle around until I'm in the same position. It *is* comfortable. I glance over at the movie cases on the shelf nearest the couch, and try to read the titles. It's hard to do while my head is upside-down.

"We need to think about this first," she declares. "What else can ghosts do?"

I ponder for a minute. I've been over this myself a million times, but I try to give it full consideration. What do I remember from Mama's tales? What do I remember from movies I've watched?

"Ghosts are supposed to be able to pass through things, like I can, and you can too. Ghosts can *move* things — but I can't. Ghosts make people who touch them cold, or they make a space cold." I think of Edward shivering yesterday, and grin. "I don't know if I make the whole room cold. I don't think so. But I definitely make whoever I touch cold."

"I haven't tried moving anything yet. I wonder how you'd do it?" Ashley looks over her head at the nearest shelf. She scrunches her face up, then relaxes, her eyebrows drawn together. "That didn't work, so I guess I can't either? So much for watching a movie tonight. What else?"

"Well … ghosts can make noise sometimes. But I can't, not that anyone can hear. I remember one movie where the ghost entered another person's body and took control of them. I can enter someone's body, but it's more like I enter the person's mind — I become them, sort of, like you saw with Savannah. But I can't control the person." I wouldn't want to, either — all I want to do when that happens is get *out*. "And, of course, ghosts often haunt a particular place, like I do. Although *you* don't seem to."

I eye her, but she seems oblivious to the pointedness of my statement.

Why is Ashley able to leave the building? Why did she come here in the first place instead of haunting the place where she died? Why is she avoiding my questions about *her*? Does she truly not know the answers, or is she just not telling me?

It's a good thing we're sprawled across the couch like this, or Ashley would see my expression. If Mama were here she'd tell me my face might freeze this way. I stare at the wall under my sneakered feet. One foot is on a movie poster for the unfortunately named film *Fred and the Magical Hot Dog Stand*; the other foot is resting on *Blood, Gore, and Mayhem*, an apt title given the level of revulsion implied by the advertisement. I move my left foot so that both feet are on Fred's poster.

"Hey, I know!" Ashley's enthusiasm interrupts my thoughts. She's probably eaten a million hot dogs in her life. With both ketchup *and* mustard, I bet.

"What?" I snap. Maybe she choked to death on a hot dog. As soon as the thought crosses my mind I feel guilty. I've had an embarrassing number of uncharitable thoughts since I met Ashley.

"What did you think of?" I say, in a much friendlier tone. It isn't very nice to think about bad things happening to someone else, even if that person is already dead. I'm irritated that she doesn't have to follow the same rules as me, but she *is* my friend.

My only friend.

Ashley has noticed none of my sulking. She stretches her arms above her head and slides off onto the carpet, managing to use her arms to catch herself right before her head smacks into the floor. I do the same thing, with significantly less grace.

We lie on the floor, our legs resting on the seat of the couch. The carpet is rather dirty. Matt usually vacuums it, but the vacuum cleaner broke a few weeks ago and Mrs. Briarwood has yet to bring the new one she promised. I bite my lip to hide the smile that threatens to appear when I think of Matt.

"You said you didn't, um, didn't die in these clothes, right?" She eyes my crisp, white T-shirt. One advantage of being a ghost is that my clothing always stays clean.

As none of what I'm wearing had been invented when I was killed, it would have been a difficult task to die in this outfit. "Right. I —" What exactly did I do? "I guess I made up these clothes. I watched what I saw other people wear, and I thought this would fit." I study my shirt, blue jeans, and white sneakers. "Does it look okay?"

I examine Ashley's clothes — she too is wearing jeans, and she's got on a pretty blue sweater. Should I be wearing a sweater instead? And her sneakers are slightly different than mine. Did I pick an unstylish design to emulate?

"You look fine. Plain, but fine."

I prop myself up on my elbows, trying not to look at my attire. Plain is okay, I suppose, especially since no one can see me. Although Ashley can, now.

"I change the color of my shirt every once in a while," I offer. Is the outfit plain or are the colors plain? My shirt was yellow for a while, then I decided yellow wasn't a good color for my complexion. I can't see myself in a mirror, so I have no way to know for sure, but I suspect it makes me look a bit sallow. I figured a white shirt would be okay, but maybe I should have stuck with yellow?

She sits up, tucking her legs underneath her as she regards me intently. "How did you make your clothes?"

"I'm sorry, Ashley; I honestly have no idea. I thought about what I should be wearing, and then I was wearing it. I've always figured this was part of being a ghost."

I also always thought that a ghost would know how it had died.

"Well," she says, conspiratorially, "here's my idea. If you can create clothes, then you can create *things!*" She beams and leans back.

"What are you talking about?" Things? What kind of things? What would I create? An automobile? A trampoline?

She looks cross. "Work with me on this, Emma. If you can create clothing, then why can't you create something else? Something that you and I could share? Like — " She muses for a moment. "Like a deck of cards!"

Have I ever tried to create something? I must have. I think back over the years.

"I tried to create a book once," I say. "But it didn't work."

"Was it a book you'd read while you were alive?"

"No."

"Maybe that's the problem. Maybe you can only create things that you interacted with when you were alive?"

We both look down at my legs, encased in modern blue denim, nothing like the fabric that jeans were made of in the 1800s. I never would have worn pants in those days anyway — Mama would have had my hide.

"Never mind," she mutters. She stands up and rests an elbow on the nearest shelf of movies.

A noise from almost directly underneath us makes me jump. It was a soft thump, like a door closing.

"Did you hear that?" I scramble to my feet. I try to picture the layout of the basement. There are some storage rooms and a laundry room, but my thoughts are suddenly in a jumble and I can't remember which room is where. The cool, dank, stone-walled cellar that is etched in my memory is from the original house, not this one.

"I didn't hear anything." Ashley's face is blank and unconcerned, her voice distant. She's staring at the wall behind me. She looks like she's inspecting the movie posters, but from her expression I think she's actually very far away.

I must have imagined the noise, but that would make two noises I've imagined from the basement tonight. It was one thing to hear sounds from below when Tim Connelly was downstairs riding his exercise bike, or when someone was in the laundry room at the foot of the stairs, but this is different. No one is in the basement. No one could be in the basement.

I know I can't be hurt because I'm already dead, but I'm afraid anyway.

I scramble on to the couch and pull my feet up. I have a sudden, irrational fear of touching the floor that is all that stands between us and the basement.

"Are you sure you didn't hear it?"

The noise sounds again. It's louder this time. I might have heard a voice. It sounded deep, a man's voice. Or it could have been the wind. A deep, male wind? I wrap my arms around my legs.

"Ashley, did you hear that?" I whisper.

"No." Her voice is soft and dreamy, and her eyes are unfocused. She leans her head to one side. "I didn't hear —"

She vanishes.

"Ashley!" I leap up and run my trembling hands through the space where she was just standing. I was watching her and then — she just wasn't there!

Another thump comes from below. This time I can feel the vibration through the floor.

"Ashley!" I sprint across the room. I don't know if I'm running to or away from something.

"Where are you?"

A sudden thunk stops me dead in my tracks. In my panic I've run smack into the nonexistent wall of the original house. Tires squeal outside as a car speeds down the street, the sound of the engine fierce and loud. I rub my forehead where I smacked it. Running about isn't going to help anything. I know what I need to do, and I need to do it now.

I turn and trudge through the store, my footsteps getting slower and slower, until I reach the one place where I might be able to figure out what is going on. The one place where I might — just might — be able to find out what the noises were, and maybe discover why Ashley keeps disappearing. Both times Ashley has disappeared there have been noises from the basement. Are they related? Could they be? How? And if I really did hear a voice … Who is downstairs? How did he — or she — get there?

I slink around the last row of movies and slide to my knees as both my energy and willpower slip away, leaving me an empty, hollow shell filled only with dread. My left hand grips the edge of the nearest shelf so hard it hurts.

Prickles run down my spine as I stare at the door to the basement.

No one ever goes down there. No one has in years. The door is closed and locked, and Mrs. Briarwood is the only one with the key.

Where is Ashley?

Six

I stare at the door, trying to work up the nerve to go through it. When I revisit the place of my death the memories smother me. Being dead doesn't make them any less dreadful. And now I'm even more afraid than normal because I'm scared of what I might find.

The warmth of the morning sun on my neck rouses me from my guilt-filled vigil. I look at the clock, then sigh and pull myself to my feet. I'm the biggest chicken ever. If I don't check the basement, then I'll be letting Ashley down. But maybe whatever made the noises isn't related to her disappearances at all? Maybe I only imagined those sounds?

I know this isn't true even as I suggest it to myself. I heard something, whether or not it is related to Ashley, and I'm allowing myself to let my fear of a man who has been dead for years keep me from investigating.

I glance out the window as I take a step closer to the door and try to think courageous thoughts. There's a woman walking her dog down the sidewalk, her coat buttoned up against the early morning chill. The dog is a cute, friendly-looking dog, big and brown, with floppy ears. She walks him past the store every morning at exactly the same time, no matter what the weather is like. I call the woman Mrs. Nesbitt — not because that's her name, of course, that's just the name I've given her. The dog I call Bruno.

"She's a bitch."

I whip around to see Ashley standing next to me, wrinkling her nose at Mrs. Nesbitt.

"Where did you come from? Are you okay?" I grab her arm as if to prove to myself that she's really here. She feels warm and solid. But I saw her disappear before, so solidity only means so much. A chill runs from the nape of my neck all the way down to my ankles.

Ashley frowns at me as if I'm crazy. "I'm fine, relax!" She pats me lightly on the shoulder, then walks over to the window. I stumble after her, my head all a whirl. Mrs. Nesbitt clomps by in her sturdy, sensible black shoes. Her white hair is almost hidden by a crimson scarf. One gloved hand is tight on Bruno's leash. His tongue is hanging out, and he looks like he's smiling.

"That's Ms. Englestadt, my English teacher. I hate her." Her voice is filled with venom.

Ashley hates Mrs. Nesbitt? Mrs. Nesbitt is Ms. Englestadt? I don't want to know Bruno's real name — he just looks like a Bruno, so I'm going to keep thinking of him as that. I watch the pair walk past the window, my mind racing.

"Ashley, *where did you go?*"

Ashley shrugs, apparently as unconcerned by her latest disappearance as she was by the previous ones. "I don't know."

How can she not know? Doesn't this matter to her? Isn't she afraid? I would be terrified.

And I am.

I tuck my hair behind my ears.

"There were noises from the basement around when you disappeared." I watch her out of the corner of my eye and try to act as if I'm looking out the window.

She sticks her tongue out at Mrs. Nesbitt. This is like when Lizzie would pretend she couldn't hear me just to make me angry. I've had enough. I turn to face her, hands on my hips.

"Ashley, did you go downstairs? Do you know what those sounds were?"

She stares out the window as if she didn't hear me. Can she hear me? Am I disappearing? I shake my head — that is ridiculous! I'm here, I'm real — as real as a ghost can be. But Ashley …

"Don't you care about this?" My voice catches. *I* care. *I'm* worried. But what am I really worried about? That she's a ghost with different rules than me, or that one day she'll disappear for good and I'll be alone again? Because even if there is someone or something, in the basement, we're both still ghosts.

I press my face against the chill of the glass and watch Mrs. Nesbitt — Mrs. Englestadt — and Bruno. They turn the corner and are gone.

"Did you have a boyfriend?" Ashley pushes her nose against the window, smushing it flat, then reaches through the glass with her left hand and pokes at her nose from the outside of the store. "Hey, check this out!"

What is wrong with her? Why won't she talk about this?

"No, I didn't," I snap. That isn't entirely true. Ned had just started calling on me, but we hadn't had much time together before I was captured. "Well, maybe," I correct myself. I suppose he was my boyfriend, if only for a day or two.

"Really?" She stops fiddling with her nose and starts poking a forefinger against the glass. First she taps the glass, then she pokes her finger through the glass, then she taps again. She's having far too much fun with this. See how she likes it after a hundred years.

"What is — I mean what was, sorry, since he's probably dead. What was his name?"

"*Probably* dead?" I snap. "He'd be 150 years old or so if he were still alive; there's no *probably* about it." How callous of her to gloss over his death like that! What if I'd been pining away for him all these years? I glare at Ashley. She looks contrite, and a little alarmed. Her forefinger is frozen in mid poke, the tip still on the outside of the window.

"His name was Ned." I suppose I did pine, but there wasn't anything I could do about it. I have a brief flash of how wonderful it felt to have his large, work-worn hand envelop mine. After all these years I still miss him something fierce.

I drag myself back to the present and cross my arms.

"What is wrong with you? I'm trying to talk to you about something important!"

"Yeah, sorry. Hey, can you do this? Isn't it cool?" She steps out through the glass entirely and waves to me from the street, then jumps back in to the store.

I grit my teeth. "No, I can't do that." I want to smack her. "I can't leave the store." Not on this side, at least, since this wall parallels the old wall.

"Why not?" She finally sees my expression and stops her antics. "Sorry, Emma. I'm just playing." She has a different top on. Yesterday her sweater was blue, but today it's light green. I'm pretty sure this is a different sweater, too — the stitching on the sleeves looks slightly more ornate. She notices my gaze.

"Don't you just love it? I wanted to buy this sweater, but it didn't fit me right. But now that I'm dead and can make up my own clothes I figured I could just imagine it fitting. And it did!" She beams.

"It's lovely," I reply, clenching my teeth. I take a deep breath and try to sound calm and convincing. "Ashley, I'd really like to talk to you about this."

"Let's talk about what's-his-name first, okay?" She smiles a little half smile. "Then we can talk about … about the other stuff. Please?" Her eyes plead with me.

I waver, then cave. If that's what it takes to get her to talk, fine.

"All right — Ned, then the other stuff. Promise?"

"Promise." She twirls around, then does a cartwheel down the nearest aisle. "Your turn, Emma!"

She seems a bit more childish today, although maybe this is her real personality — I've only known her for a day. "Um, I'll try, but I've never done that before."

"Really? Why not?" She does another cartwheel, then another. I used to watch Katie and her girlfriends do these on the lawn, back when there was grass on the side of the house instead of a parking lot.

"I don't know, I just didn't." I can just imagine Papa catching me flipping around in mid-spin, my skirts bunched around my waist and my legs in the air.

"So tell me about Ned!"

I stand still, staring at the floor. I have to put down first one hand, then the other, and keep my body in a straight line when my legs are in the air. That doesn't seem too hard. Conceptually.

"He lived down the road. His family homesteaded just like mine, and we knew each other since we were little." Ned's family moved here the same year we did, all of us brought to Colorado by the government's promise of 160 acres to anyone who would live on the land and farm it for five years. Ned must have married some other girl, since I was obviously no longer available. Did he settle down and get his own 160 acres? Did he love the woman he married as much as he loved me?

I take a deep breath, then make my first ever acrobatic attempt. My right hand lands solidly, then my left hand, then —

I lose my balance and fall sideways, my legs vanishing into the rack of movies. It looked so straightforward when Ashley did it. I lie there and stare at the area where my body disappears and the shelf begins.

"So how far did you go?"

I turn my head to the left. I'm about five feet from where I started. "Not very far. I fell over." I slide my legs back out of the shelf, then put my hands under my head and stare at the ceiling. Did I lift my legs off of the ground too soon?

"I mean with Ned!" Ashley cartwheels back down the aisle. I cringe as I realize she's going to land on me, then she goes *through* me instead of touching me. "Ha! You thought I was going to run into you!"

I wish I could throw something at her. I get up and make another attempt at a cartwheel, ending up in roughly the same position. Maybe I'm going too fast? Or too slow?

"So did you kiss him? Or ..." her voice trails off suggestively.

"We kissed." I remember the kiss well. I was so nervous. Ned had driven Lizzie and me home after we spent the day working on his sister's marriage quilt with the other girls from the area. She was marrying a man from Denver and was fretting about moving away, so Lizzie and I stayed later than we'd expected so we could console her, and it was dark by the time we got home. Ned helped us both down from the wagon, then Lizzie ran into the house, leaving us alone for a brief moment. I don't remember how it happened exactly, just that suddenly our mouths were pressed together as if the world were about to end. His lips were soft and warm, firm yet supple against my own. I felt so safe in his arms, wrapped up inside his embrace, encircled by the protection of his strength.

"And?"

One kiss, that's all we had time for. One wonderful, beautiful kiss.

"That's it. We kissed just the once." I try another cartwheel and land flat on my back. Could he have possibly married Beverly? I hope not. She was a little too fussy for him and would probably have driven him batty.

"Oh." Ashley sounds disappointed, as if I've let her down by not having had a steamy relationship. Doesn't she realize I grew up in the 1800s? Not that I was a prude, and I heard plenty of racy stories from Beverly about what her cousins did on dates in the city. But out in the plains where we lived it wouldn't have been proper to do too much with a man unless he was your husband.

"Well, I got captured the next day," I snap. "I would have liked to kiss him more than once."

"I'm sorry." She watches me ready myself for another attempt, my arms outstretched, my hands in the air. "Wait, let me help you." She comes over and stands next to me.

"You're starting off just fine, but you're letting your balance shift too fast when you start to move forward. Try it again, but try to remember to distribute your weight evenly. Think of it as keeping your entire body in a single line." She gestures with her hand in case I don't know where the line should be.

"That's what I've been trying to do!" Although she may have a point about the weight part. I take a breath, make myself into a big X with my arms and legs outstretched, then fling myself forward, concentrating hard on keeping my limbs lined up. It can't look pretty, but I manage my first successful cartwheel.

"I did it!" I feel a ridiculously strong sense of accomplishment.

Ashley claps her hands together. "That was great!" She's smiling, either because she's proud of me or because I'm entertaining. I decide to pretend it's the former.

I try another cartwheel, and squeak through with the same lack of grace. I would surely be out of breath, if I still was able to breathe. "This must be easier to learn when you're alive!"

She shrugs. "I suppose it is easier to learn things like that when you know your body is real. It's not like you're going to hurt yourself now. Want to try a back flip?"

What on earth is a back flip? Whatever it is, I bet it's harder than a cartwheel. I open my mouth to respond.

A jingle from the front door signals Vicki's arrival, and I snap my mouth shut. Ashley and I peer over the racks of videos to watch her. Vicki walks in, carrying a stack of schoolbooks and a very large handbag.

"Dammit, Matt!" she growls, and kicks the door shut behind her. Matt is supposed to open the store every weekday at ten. He probably makes it here on time once every three weeks.

"Who is Matt?" Ashley whispers.

"The fellow who was supposed to open the store," I whisper back. "Why are you whispering?"

"So she doesn't hear us," Ashley replies, then grins and raises her voice. "Habit, I guess." She watches Vicki bustle around behind the counter, grumbling to herself about Matt. "Hey, I think I'm going to go see if I've been found."

"No! You promised to talk with me about your disappearances if I told you about Ned." I'm not letting her off the hook this time. Enough is enough.

"I know, and I will. But —" She sniffles and glances out the window. "I really feel I should go see. Plus everyone is probably sad because I'm dead. It won't take long. My house isn't very far from here." A tear trickles down her face and she brushes it away. "Please, Emma? I just … I just need to go see."

I can't very well argue with this. At least she can go see how her family is taking her death. My chest tightens at the prospect of her leaving again. What if she doesn't come back? Although even when she vanishes inexplicably she always comes back. Also inexplicably.

Or at least she's always come back so far.

"Oh ... fine. But we're talking when you get back!" I furrow my brow and attempt to look stern.

"Are you *sure* you can't leave the store? I'd really like you to come with me."

"Yes." I try to keep my voice level in spite of my frustration. Of course I'm sure. "I've been trying since before your grandparents were born."

"Oh, right." She looks out the window, then back at me. "Will you be okay here by yourself?"

Will *I* be okay?

"I've had a lot of practice."

"Okay, I'll be back!" She smiles and leaps through the window, waves merrily to me, then heads down the street.

I press my hands flat on the glass and watch her stroll down the sidewalk, past the card shop next door, then past the other stores on the street. I don't know what any of those shops sell because I can't see them from here. If I could leave the building I would know, but I can't.

My body aches with envy, and my heart feels the coldness of fear.

~~~~~

Matt shows up around eleven. He must have switched shifts with Stacia because she was scheduled for this morning.

He's nothing at all like Ned. Ned was tall, his skin dark from time in the sun, and freckled; he had broad shoulders, his muscles strong from working on the farm. Matt's skin is pale, and his body is much more defined — but his muscles are from exercising in a gym. Ned had reddish-brown hair, thick and straight; Matt's is a golden brown, his head a tangled mop of curls. Ned's eyes were a rich, warm brown. Matt's are a piercing grayish-blue.

Personality-wise they're also very different. Ned was a hard worker, whereas Matt is what people these days call a "slacker." Ned didn't have the chance to go to college, but Matt did. For some reason Matt never finished. I don't know why, but I heard him say that to someone once. Ned was generous to a fault — Matt is lazy and selfish.

On the other hand, he is also incredibly charismatic. I watch as he compliments Vicki's hair, asks her how her classes are going, and flashes that incredible smile of his until she's not only forgotten that he was an hour late for work, but she offers to come in early Monday morning and open the store for him. His power is like that of a siren — inexplicable and irresistible.

Do I like Matt as much as I do merely because he's here? Would I fall for his charm if I was alive, or is my affection for him manufactured for the sake of convenience?

No matter. Unless he suddenly becomes a ghost there's really nothing to be gained. And there's nothing to be lost either. I follow Matt around the store like a schoolgirl, wallowing in my crush while I wait for Ashley to return. He's straightening the shelves, and making sure all the movies are filed correctly. Even through my rose-colored vision I know that he's only doing this because he doesn't want to work at the counter. Fortunately for Vicki it's a slow day.

Savannah appears in late afternoon. Her long blonde hair sparkles in the fluorescent lights. Her sweater is quite snug in the bosom, but on her the tightness is attractive, not tawdry. Her high-heeled boots add a grown-up, stylish touch. She looks much more sophisticated than her fifteen or so years.

Matt is drawn to her like a moth to a flame.

He abandons the stack of movies he's been re-shelving, leaving them in a small pile in Comedy. Savannah has clearly noticed him, but doesn't want him to realize that she has, and he is doing exactly the same thing. The pretense at nonchalance on both their parts is amusing to me, their invisible spectator. He's tall enough to see her easily over the rows of shelves, and he times his stride so that he intersects her path right as she reaches the end of the aisle.

A hot stab of jealousy tightens my chest, but I swallow and try to stifle it. It's foolish to be jealous when I'm technically not even in the same plane of existence. I lean against the wall next to them as they make small talk. I watch, spellbound, as he says exactly the right things at exactly the right time to make Savannah feel as if she's the most important thing in his world.

"Oh shit!" A wail from the front of the store pulls my eyes away. Vicki has just spilled her drink all over the countertop. I realize my hands are clenched tight, and that my fingernails are digging into my palms.

I'm not doing very well at convincing myself I'm not jealous.

The distraction pulls me out of my Matt-obsession long enough for me to realize how late it is. Where is Ashley? She's been gone for most of the day.

I glance around the store. An elderly couple is tottering down one aisle, three children are hassling Vicki about a scratched DVD while she tries to mop up the countertop, and Edward is lurking by the stack of used movies for sale. I bet he came here to ogle Stacia because she normally works on Friday afternoons.

A blue and white bandana is tied around his head. Long, chocolate-colored hair hangs down his back. His eyes are hidden behind dark glasses with a silver metal frame. The back of his black leather jacket is emblazoned with the words "Harley-Davidson," and his boots are made from black leather as well. A chain hangs from his waistband, and he has thick silver studs on both his boots and on a leather band worn on his left wrist. His left ear sports three separate earrings, all large, silver, and shiny. I don't think he's shaved in several days. He is tall and broad-shouldered, and with his size and his biker getup, he's a big and intimidating man. Whenever he's here the other customers step out of his way.

His eyes are hidden behind the dark glass, but his face is turned toward Savannah. I can tell he's watching her while she and Matt continue their dance of flirtation. I don't like the way he stares at Stacia, and I don't like the way he is watching Savannah. What if he's thinking the same kind of things about Savannah that he thought about Stacia when I touched him the other day? I shudder and rub my left wrist. What horrible thoughts. What a horrible man.

I scowl at him through narrowed eyes. He reminds me of my murderer, who also had long, brown hair, although Edward's is significantly cleaner, and Edward does have much better teeth. But it's more than that. Edward looks like the kind of guy who could do bad things to people, who could destroy someone's life without a second thought.

A creepy crawly feeling spreads across my shoulders, like a spider running lightly across my skin.

What if Edward *is* a murderer?

What if he killed Ashley?

I watch him watch Savannah. He's pretending to look through the used DVDs. He grabs each one from the shelf with his thick fingers, turns it over, then puts it back on the shelf. He glances at them so quickly that there's no way he's really reading anything. He stops and looks at his watch, then sets the last movie down and heads toward the door. His heavy booted feet clomp on the floor. I shadow him, my own feet soundless, a shadow without even a shadow of my own.

As he passes Savannah he bumps into her and mutters, "Pardon me." She eyes him and takes a step back, even though he keeps moving. I stop near her and rest a hand on the shelf next to me. His voice is deep and gruff. And low, like the voice I heard from downstairs.

Could Edward have been down there last night? Could he have broken into the store and slipped down into the basement while I was up on the second floor?

Vicki walks toward the back of the store, a stack of movie cases in her arms. As she passes Edward her steps slow, then she stops and stares at his back, her eyes narrowed, as he continues on. As he saunters past the basement door he taps the wood twice with his thick knuckles, and then he's out the main door. A minute later a motorcycle engine revs from the parking lot, and a loud rumbling follows as he drives away. Vicki shakes her head and heads toward the counter.

Why did he knock on the door to the basement? He's never done that before — but I've never heard noises from the basement before either! Did Edward kill Ashley? Is he planning to kill Stacia too? Or Savannah? Or both of them?

I feel myself trembling as I look at the door that is all that stands between me and the place of my death. I have to go down there. This isn't like when I make myself go downstairs to walk the boundaries. I have to see if Ashley's body is there. If it is —

I swallow. If it is, there won't be anything I'll be able to do except tell Ashley. I won't be able to make her alive again any more than I could do the same for myself. And there's nothing I'll be able to do to stop Edward next time. Nothing at all. I can't save Stacia, or Savannah, or anyone else he decides to kill.

I'm just a ghost. I can't *do* anything.

I squeeze past Savannah and stare at the door. The brown wood was long ago painted over with white, the paint now peeling in places. The crystal doorknob is covered with dust, its brass base tarnished. It hasn't been polished in years.

But polished or not, dusty or not, I don't need to use it.

I take a deep breath, clench my hands into fists, then step through the door itself.

Seven

I stop just inside the door, on the small landing at the top of the stairs, and crinkle my nose. The air smells old and stale. My eyes flit around the enclosed space. I'm standing on the old pine floor; the gray carpet ends at the doorway. A sliver of light peeks underneath the wooden door, its feeble glow emphasizing, not illuminating, the darkness on this side. There is a thick layer of dust on the floorboards, the trim, and on the railings on either side of the steps. I don't think anyone alive has come down here for at least two years, maybe three.

I peer down the narrow staircase, my eyes wide as can be, and try to will myself to stop shaking. I can do this. I've gone down these steps a million times to check the boundaries.

I wrap my arms around myself, but I don't feel any less frightened. Maybe I should ask Ashley to go downstairs instead? No, that wouldn't be right. And what would I say, anyway? I think your corpse is in the basement, you might want to go take a look?

Matt's voice moves across the room behind me, his rich tones growing louder and louder until he stops just outside the door. All the sounds from the store are muffled, as though I'm hearing them through pillows held against both my ears.

"Until later, " he says. His deep voice is melodious, like a fairytale voice that could put you under a spell if you listened to it for very long. There's a soft, higher-pitched reply from someone, although I can't make out the words, then I hear the jingle of the bells on the front door. The smitten Savannah must have left.

Any jealousy I might have felt is smothered by fear.

This staircase is in the same place as the stairs were in the original house, but they look completely different. The old stairs were stone, cold and hard and uneven. These are wooden, each worn down slightly in the middle from years of use, and there are walls on both sides of the steps instead of just on the one side. The old stairs didn't even have a railing; there was open space on the right side and a stone wall on the left.

I peer down the dark stairwell, then run my eyes over the wall next to me. There is a series of lines etched into the wood. The Petersons used to measure the heights of their kids here, and seeing each height and name brings a quavering smile to my lips in spite of my nervousness.

I remember when Katie was that small, and there — there's the year when Jimmy passed his mother in height. It's funny how I have such strong memories of each of them at different stages of their lives. Little Katie with her baby dolls, teenage Katie sneaking out her bedroom window at night, and grownup Katie coming home to visit with her own children; Jimmy running around the house, pulling the cat's tail, making faces at that awful parrot, sneaking cookies when his mom wasn't looking — and then later going off to the war he never believed in and never returned from. And here is the record of how they grew, preserved long after they themselves are gone.

I watched them from my ghostly state, envying their lives even as I savored seeing them grow. They felt almost like members of my own family, as did the Nelsons and the Connellys. I loved every one of them. I worried when they were sick, I was sad when they were troubled. I fretted when Jimmy went off to war, and I sat with his parents when they got the call, ghostly tears running down my face just like the real tears on theirs.

I watched Shannon Connelly fall out of the old maple tree and break her arm, and I was almost as ecstatic as she was when it healed up just in time for her to take the ballet class she'd been waiting for. I learned how to knit, in concept if not in practice, from paying close attention while Maude knitted outfits for all her babies, and I cried along with her every time she miscarried. I watched the children turn into grownups, watched the parents grow old. I shared their lives, and treasured the experience, even though they never knew of my existence.

I run my fingers over the names on the wall. Whatever happened to the children of the children I knew? Where are they all now? If I suddenly became alive I'd be a stranger in spite of the fact of all I know about them.

Someone in the store laughs, the happy sound dampened by its travel through the solid wooden door.

All I am is a spectator. A voyeur. The only person who knows *me*, who knows I'm here at all, is Ashley.

The dark maw below beckons.

I take one faltering step down, slow and tentative as I place my foot carefully on the narrow wooden step. I'm a ghost. Nothing can possibly happen to me.

I don't convince myself.

I grasp the railings on either side of me, both hands wrapped tight around the wood worn smooth through years of use. The air is stale and dusty, but I can smell the dankness of the old cellar. The step feels light under my feet, and at the same time thick and heavy, as I feel both the thin wooden step of today and the rough-hewn stone one of the past. I force myself to place my other foot on the next stair, every part of my body and soul resisting, screaming at me to *turn! Go back! Don't go down these stairs!*

Lizzie's face pops into my mind, with her greenish-brown eyes, a smattering of freckles across her nose, and her long, thick, curly brown hair. My own hair is much more fine — I always envied her thick hair. Ashley doesn't look like Lizzie in the least, except for her eyes, but she definitely reminds me of my little sister. I'm awfully glad it was me that was caught and killed, not Lizzie.

I glance over my shoulder at the door, a dim, dark rectangle in the grayness of the stairwell. I could go back through it right now. I don't have to do this. I don't have to go downstairs. If Ashley's body is there she'll find out soon enough, won't she?

I can suggest that she look in the basement. I can figure out a way to bring it up so that she thinks it's her idea.

I swallow. If it were Lizzie, I would go down to find out if her body was there so I could spare her the horror of finding it on her own. Ashley isn't my sister, but she doesn't have anyone else but me. And I don't have anyone else but her.

I screw my eyes shut and force myself down one more step. I feel like I'm walking through thick mud, the kind where your feet stick and you have to pull really hard to jerk them loose. I slide my hands along both railings, keeping my grip tight, afraid to touch the wall on my left because I know if I do I'll feel the stones that have been replaced by plaster. I can smell them, the damp, moist rock scent strong in my nostrils even though the stairwell is dusty and dry.

I never actually walked down the stone steps I can feel under my feet.

~~~~~

I was unconscious when he carried me to the house. He had to have waited until Nate and his son went away before picking me up, because they would have seen us for sure if they'd only turned around. He must've dragged me for a mile by my arms. When I came to my shoulders were sore, my arms felt like they had nearly been pulled out of their sockets, and my skirts were ripped to shreds and stuck full with burrs and prickly pear needles. I woke up lying on my left side on the hard wooden planks just inside the door to the house. My arms were tied together in front of me, the frayed rope he'd knotted tight around my wrists digging into my skin. My boots were missing, and my legs were bound at the ankles. The back of my head hurt, and a scrape on the right side of my face stung as if I were being pricked with a thousand pins.

It was almost dark outside, the daylight fading as the sun eased behind the mountains. A soft, rosy glow grew fainter as I looked through the one window I could see. The only light inside the house was from a wood fire burning in the rough stone fireplace. The glow from the flames felt harsh and forbidding, unlike the cheery, welcoming fire at my family's house.

He crouched on the other side of the room, stirring something in a greasy black kettle that hung over the flames. It smelled like rabbit stew, which was normally a favorite of mine, but the aroma made me want to vomit. I felt like a rabbit myself, caught in a snare. I tried to move my wrists apart, but the rope was tied far too tight for me to even attempt to get out of it, and I couldn't manage to get my fingers on the knot.

Long, scraggly hair fell in a tangle down his back, the color a dark brown lightly streaked with gray. He was tall and lanky, even somewhat scrawny, but in spite of this he gave off the impression of raw might. Kind of like a bear waking up after hibernating all winter — lean and hungry, filled with a dangerous strength. He looked over at me, and our eyes met. A jolt of fear ran through my body like lightning, and I tried again to pull my arms free, but the knot held tight and firm. My eyes darted around the room. It was bare, empty except for the kettle and the two of us. I had no idea where I was. I'd never been in the house before and didn't recognize it at all. I could tell by the size of the room and the quality of the workmanship that it was a large, well-crafted house, but that was it.

He grinned and spat a hunk of chewing tobacco on the floor; the teeth he wasn't missing were stained a sour yellowish-brown. He stopped stirring the stew and set down the wooden spoon he was using. As he laid it next to the pot I realized it was just a stick, not a spoon. He limped slightly, favoring his left leg as he walked over to me. Again I thought I'd seen him before — but where? Who was he?

"You shouldn't of run away from me," he announced. He squatted down next to me. I squirmed away from him, then bumped into the wall. The front door was right behind my back. I could feel a cool draft blowing in from underneath the door. A trickle of sweat ran down my back. He reached out and stroked my scraped cheek with his filthy fingers. I jerked back from his touch as if his hand were a branding rod. He grabbed my face with both hands and held it tight, then rubbed my wound with his thumb, pressing hard on my injured skin.

I tried to squeeze out of his grip, but he was much stronger than me. "Let me go!" I demanded, hoping I sounded firm in spite of the fact that I could feel myself shaking.

He laughed. "And why on earth would I do that, little missy? I captured you all fair and square." He released my face abruptly. The side of my head smacked into the hard floor with a loud thunk. I felt lightheaded and blinked a few times to clear my vision. His tone altered, becoming deep and sonorous. "Like prey to the lion." He spread his hands expansively, like this all made perfect sense, as if I was his well-earned catch after a hard day's hunt.

Fair and square? What was fair about this? And how dare he compare himself to a creature as noble as the lion? A pathetic, mangy, flea-bitten lion, that's what he would be!

"My pa will be out looking for me," I said fiercely. "And he *will* find you, so you'd better let me go right now."

But how would Papa find me? Where was I?

He began to stroke my hair with his right hand, his left hand holding my shoulder firm so I couldn't roll away from his grip. I kicked my feet at him, and he moved with unexpected speed, using his legs to pin me down. He chuckled.

"I'm not letting you go, dearie." He pressed his face closer to mine. His breath smelled like rotting cabbage. "And no one is going to find you," he whispered in my ear. His hand trailed down my face, along my side, and across my hips. I shrank back from his touch.

He picked me up and threw me over his shoulder as if I were a sack of potatoes. My head thumped against his back as he walked across the room. I thrashed and twisted, curled my hands into fists and hit him as hard as I could, but it was as though I was a flea biting a giant dog. Strands of his long, dirty hair stuck to the blood on my face as he carried me through a small door, then down a flight of stone steps into the dark, dank cellar. The air smelled earthy, and it was chilly — much cooler than upstairs. He tossed me on top of a pile of straw in the middle of the dirt floor. Pieces of straw pricked my back and legs. I pushed up with my elbow and rose to my knees, but he kicked me hard in the chest with a sharp booted foot and I fell flat on my back in the straw. He struck a match and lit a lantern that hung from a beam above my head; the light brightened his cheekbones but left deep hollows under his eyes. He leered at me.

"I want to see you, girl. All of you. You're mine now." His coarse laughter echoed off the cold, damp stone walls.

I never watch movies in which women are raped.

~~~~~

My breathing is loud in the enclosed stairwell. I know it's really making no noise at all, just like I know I'm not really breathing, but it sounds loud to me nonetheless. I glance back at the door — I've only gone down three steps. Great. At this rate I might make it to the bottom by the time Edward has murdered his next victim. Could he really be murdering people here, underneath the store? How could he possibly get down there without me noticing? He is at the store all the time, lurking about like a miscreant, but I've never seen him go through the basement door. No one ever goes through the door — they would have to unlock it first, and since Mrs. Briarwood has the only key I'm sure I would notice that because she's hardly ever here! And —

I pause, my fear momentarily forgotten. The floor of the landing at the top of the stairs was thick with dust, and if someone had been through the door there would have at least been footsteps in the dust. That means no one could have come down these steps after all. Edward couldn't have murdered Ashley here, even if he managed to go through the door without me noticing him — and there's no way I would have missed him lugging her body. I turn and look up at the top of the stairs. The dim light squeezing underneath the door from the store glows like a bright beacon in the darkness.

But then there were those noises, and that voice. Was it really a voice, or was that my imagination? Maybe, but there were sounds, that's for sure, and someone made them. Someone or something. Could it have been a rat? A big spider? I shudder. It couldn't be a person making those noises, not unless there was another way in to the basement. And it would have to be an awfully large spider to make a sound that could shake the wooden floor! But there was no other way in. Was there?

My breath catches as I remember there *is* another entrance.

The original house was a well-built, roomy farmhouse, with a cellar large enough to store blocks of ice, as well as potatoes and other things that would keep for a long time. The Nelsons bought the land many years later, long after the old house had gotten struck by lighting and burned down. They extended the basement past the old cellar walls because the original foundation was unstable on the west side, which is why there is a part of the basement as well as a part of the main house that I can't go to because it wasn't part of the building I was killed in. They also put an entrance to the basement on the outside of the house. I can't reach that side of the house, and so can't reach that entrance at all. I'd almost forgotten it existed. Anyone could use that door to come and go as they pleased, and unless they were loud I would never be aware they were there at all.

"Dang it!" I squeeze my hands tight around the railings. That must be how Edward got in to the basement. And that's why I didn't know about it.

If he did kill Ashley, if her body really is here in this house, that would explain why she showed up here in the first place. If that's true I'll find her body below, and I'll tell her, so at least she'll know what happened. But what if he keeps killing people? I stomp one foot against the step I'm standing on. Oh, why can't I move things like ghosts in movies can? Why can't I do anything to stop him? If I could do nothing more than leave a note for someone, he could be caught. In one of Matt's favorite movies there are spirits who leave messages on a mirror in blood. I've always thought that was disgusting, but I would do it right now if I could.

I turn away from the faint light and back toward the bottom of the stairs. At the very least, I can find out if Ashley really was murdered here. Better for her to know what happened than to keep on wondering. I think.

I picture Ashley and me, haunting this house together, helplessly watching Edward kill one young girl after another, our collection of ghostly friends increasing.

And all I'll be able to do is watch.

I set my jaw and walk down the rest of the steps, my footsteps making no sound on the thin wooden boards.

Eight

I pause on the last step, my hands holding tight to the railings. I've been here a million times, but the fear never goes away. It grows as I walk down the stairs, and feels like pebbles collecting deep in my gut — a new pebble of fear joins with each step. Being down here is frightening enough when I'm walking my boundaries, but the fear I feel now is much, much worse. Behind one of these doors I might find Ashley's body.

It's all I can do to make myself step onto the concrete floor. My feet feel as if they are made of lead, and my arms are covered in goose bumps. I reach the first door and rest my hands flat against it. The texture is different from that of the doors upstairs. Like everything else it looks gray to me without any light, but from the feel of the wood against my skin I can tell that it hasn't been painted like they have. I run my fingers down the slightly rough surface, trying to work up the nerve to move through it. In my mind I can see Ashley's lifeless body lying on the floor behind the door; she's curled up in a ball, a rope tied tight around her neck. Are her hands tied like mine were? Or are her fingers clamped on the rope, frozen in place in a last futile attempt to save herself?

I start as I realize my hands are wrapped protectively around my own neck. I can't let my fear get the best of me — I have to do this!

I take a breath and go through the door.

I walk past the deep sink to my left, and step around the pipes poking out of the wall. A large drain sits in the middle of the floor. There is a small window above the pipes, and light shines through from the street outside — not much light, though. I peek under the sink, but there's nothing there but a rusty nail.

A small stack of cardboard boxes sits in one corner. I poke around them, but find no dead bodies. I sigh, relieved, but my task isn't over yet. I go back through the laundry room door and make myself slide through the southern door and into the hallway before I have a chance to think about what I'm doing.

There are three rooms off of the short, L-shaped hallway. One of the smaller rooms was used to store coal, and the other held ice; both eventually became simple storage areas. The third room is significantly larger; originally it was used for keeping winter vegetables and such, then the Petersons turned it into a playroom for their children. The old coal room is straight in front of me, the door wide open. I inch up to the doorway and peer in.

The wooden shelves that the Petersons put in so many years ago are still standing. I scan the room, examining every shelf. There are a few cardboard boxes here and there. I can't tell what's in them, but none of them looks large enough for a whole body. A chill runs down the back of my neck. What if Ashley's body has been cut up into little bits? How can I find her, or the pieces of her, if that's what happened?

I rush up to the nearest box and reach out to touch it, then pull my hands back. Wouldn't there be a smell if there were a dismembered body in this room? I wrinkle my nose and sniff. The room smells like it always does, dry and a little earthy. But — Edward could have chopped her body up into tiny pieces, then put each piece into a plastic bag and sealed it in a box. It wouldn't smell then, at least not right away. I grimace. Maybe I could put my hand in and feel around?

I run my fingers through my hair and take a deep breath. It's unlikely that Ashley has been killed, cut up into pieces, then packaged up in a collection of boxes and placed in a storage room in the same house that she was murdered in. And even if that is what happened, I can't just stick my hand in and feel around. That's not how being a ghost works. If I move through something I can't feel it. If I could I would be feeling the inside of the racks that the movies are stored on upstairs, or see the inside of a wall when I move through it, and I don't. When I pass through something it's as if that thing wasn't there at all. But maybe —

Maybe I could reach into a box that had empty space, then the part of my hand that was in that emptiness could feel whatever else was in the box. What would plastic-encased body parts feel like? Soft and squishy? Gooey? With hard bits where the bones are? I picture Edward gnawing like a dog on one of Ashley's bones while he squeezes bits of her into little plastic bags. It's a good thing there's nothing inside me to vomit up.

I kneel down in front of the cardboard box. It's pretty big, about two feet across, and could certainly hold a whole arm. Maybe two. I gulp, then grip the edge of the box in my left hand and place my right hand against the stiff cardboard side. My breaths are short and sharp. I feel as though I've just been chased by a mountain lion.

This is ridiculous. Nothing can hurt me — I'm already dead. And if Ashley, or part of her, is in this box … Well, she's certainly not going to feel any more pain. It'll just be a little — a little gruesome, is all.

It's a good thing I don't need to breathe because I'm breathing so fast I probably wouldn't be getting any oxygen.

I jam my hand inside the box.

The sensation is bizarre. Bits of my hand feel something, but mostly I feel a lack of touch, like when I've been inside a piece of furniture. But is that really what I feel? I try to piece together an image of what I'm touching, terrified that part of it is Ashley — *no, please let it not be Ashley* — while some cool, emotionless part of me realizes that I probably have felt the same kind of thing when I've been *in* things before, like when I've gone through walls and furniture. I've just never paid attention, is all. Wherever there's a pocket of air I must feel whatever is there, but I was never *trying* to feel things the way I am now.

Two of my fingers touch something soft and cool.

I jerk my hand out of the box as if I've been burned. Was that her? *Oh no, oh please no!* How am I going to tell her she's been hacked to pieces and packed away in the basement? I shudder and hold my breath, trying to calm down my frenzied non-breathing. If that's what happened — *please, let it not be, oh please!* — I would have to tell her. But I have to be sure, I have to — oh, this is horrible, but I have to know that what I'm touching is Ashley.

For the first time it occurs to me that there could be more than one person's bits in these boxes.

I look over my left shoulder, away from the box. My eyes see the old plaster wall but my mind visualizes the contents of the box. An elbow. Three hands. A bag full of eyeballs. I stare at the wall and thrust my hand back into the box, wriggling my fingers around until I touch the cool softness from before. Is it an eyeball? A — an organ, maybe a liver? I gag, but manage to keep my hand in the box. There isn't much room around whatever it is, but I rub my fingers over it. It's soft and small and smooth. It's round, and there are some pointy things near it. I lift my hand up and feel nothing. Either there is something really solid there, or there's a bit of empty space above the round thing. I move my hand down again but I've moved a bit to the side without realizing it and I bump into the pointy things. And then I know what I've found.

Jacks.

And a rubber ball. Not an eyeball.

I turn my head to look at the box.

There's a thick layer of dust on the top of the cardboard. This box hasn't been opened for years.

I scowl at the box, then jump up and look at the box to my right. Also dusty! I inspect all the boxes in the room. All of them are so dusty there's no way they could hold Ashley's body parts — they haven't been opened for ages!

I glare at the boxes, then scurry back out into the hallway. The door to the next storage room is slightly ajar. I grab on to the wooden trim around the doorframe and crane my neck to look in. There is an old, brown, rather musty carpet on the floor that reaches almost, but not quite, to the sides of the room. At its edges I can see the concrete that lies underneath. There are stacks upon stacks of old newspapers and magazines lined up against one wall, a broken armchair in one corner, and an old exercise bike. I don't see anything suspicious, although I can't see what's behind the half-open door. I take a few slow steps forward, then peek around the edge of the door.

There's nothing there.

I release the breath I didn't know I was holding. One more room to go.

I shuffle back into the hall, my feet slowing with each step, then stop and stare at the doorway to the last room. The door is open; the entrance beckons to me.

This room is the most likely one for Ashley's body to be in because it's where the outside entrance is. I should have thought to search it first. I hate being in this room worst of all. When I walk the boundaries down here I move as quickly as I can; I'm thorough in my attempt to find a way out, but I never linger. Especially not in this room.

I close my eyes and clench my hands into fists. A soft creak sounds from above; someone must have stepped on a loose board upstairs. I unclench my hands, stretching my fingers straight. I have to find out if Ashley's body is really down here. And if she is, then there's only one place she can be.

I force my eyes open and focus on my sneakered feet, the newfangled shoes bright white in the grayness of the basement. I lift up one suddenly heavy foot and make myself take one step forward, then another. When I reach the entrance I glance up for a second, into the darkness of the room in front of me, then look back down at my sneakers and walk through the opening. My heart is thumping madly away, and my steps falter when I'm just a few paces in from the doorway. I wrap my arms around myself and stare at the carpeted floor, the dull brown yet another shade of gray to me in the darkness. It's all I can do to not run back upstairs.

I know this section of the house well.

I lay on the pile of dirty straw, curled up into as tight a ball as I could with my wrists and ankles bound like they were. The remnants of my tattered dress left much of my skin exposed, and I shivered in the cool air. He'd shut the door at the top of the stairs, and I couldn't see anything now that it was nighttime — the little bit of light that shone in under the door during the day was gone. Everything was black, the darkness thick around me. I felt something run across my foot and I whimpered, but I didn't scream. I'd quickly learned to be quiet.

The room I remember from the past now extends for an extra nine or ten feet to the west. The stone walls on that side are gone, the others covered up with plaster and drywall, with wood paneling on top of that. The wall behind me wasn't there in the old house. The old stairs looked so forbidding, the stone an inflexible, impenetrable barrier between me and escape. I would lie here on the floor and stare at the steps, wishing he would leave the house long enough for me to scale them. He never did.

I crept across the hard dirt floor, pulling myself forward with my forearms, then dragging my knees along behind. The coarse rope pinched at my wrists and ankles. It was slow going. The damp soil was cold under my bare arms, the scent of moist earth strong. My stomach growled, angry at its emptiness. He fed me only once a day. I didn't want to eat at first, then realized that the only way I would be able to escape was if I kept my strength up. He always made sure to spit in my food right in front of me.

There are two small windows, one on the west wall and one on the south. The vaguest hint of light trickles through the dirty panes. There's a big wicker rocking chair to my left, but I can't see underneath it. I swallow, then walk over to the chair and crouch down to peek under it. There's nothing there. I stand up and take a trembling step back, then lose my balance and bump into the wall behind me. A nail digs into my side, and the smooth, painted surface under my fingers mingles with the hard stones of the old wall in my memory, the stones I know lie underneath this wall, the wall of the present.

I press my back against the wall and splay my shanking hands flat across the paneling. He's not here. He died long ago — he's not here. My legs feel weak and wobbly, and there's a sharp pain in my chest. I take a deep breath. I'm already dead. He killed me once — but he can't hurt me now.

The stones are cold under my fingers.

I step away from the wall within a wall and run trembling hands through my hair. I slide one foot across the carpet. As in the last room, the carpet covers the cement floor, which covers the earthen one that I knew.

I reached the wall and followed it to the left, toward the foot of the stairs, bumping my right shoulder into the wall as I crawled so that I wouldn't lose my way in the darkness and wander off into the middle of the room. The iciness of the stones rubbed against my bare skin. Why had no one found me yet? Weren't they looking? They had to be — Papa wouldn't let me disappear without searching and searching. Our community was small, but everyone knew everyone else, and we all looked out for each other. But they hadn't come here yet. Sound carried right through the floorboards above, and I would have heard something for sure. Why had no one looked here?

Tiny rocks dug into my knees as I shuffled forward, but I had to ignore the pain; I couldn't make any noise that he might hear. At this hour he would be asleep. He had to be. If I could manage to crawl up the stairs, I could escape. I just had to be quiet, so very quiet. I would climb up the steps, open the door, and sneak out of the house. But then what would I do? It had to be a mile or two to the closest homestead. I would never be able to get that far. And worse, what if I couldn't get out at all because the door was locked? My left knee landed on something sharp and I gasped, biting my lip hard to keep from crying out.

I scan the room, looking for what I'm afraid I'll find. Normally I don't pay much mind to the things I see down here. I focus on my boundaries, searching for a way out, then when I admit to myself that there isn't one, as there never is, I dash back up the stairs as if the devil himself were chasing me. But this time is different. This time I have to take the time to really look.

The Connelly children were too overwhelmed at losing their elderly parents in that horrible car accident to care about things that had already spent years gathering dust in the basement, and Mrs. Briarwood didn't bother to do anything about them when she bought the house, so the same clutter has been here for so long that there's a solid layer of dust covering everything. I recognize the old striped sofa along the south wall. The Connellys used to keep it in the living room until their kids jumped on it one day and the springs broke. Several piles of books lie in the northeast corner, next to an old television set with rabbit ears resting on top of it. Some rags or blankets lie near the west wall, near an old set of weights. There's an old mattress on a wooden bedframe in the southwest corner.

The rock underneath my right shoulder disappeared. The steps were lower now, and I was almost at the bottom of the stairs. I stopped crawling, then lifted my arms and used my elbows to leverage myself onto the stones, then up one step, then another.

I managed to climb up several more stairs before I heard a noise from above — a sharp, echoing creak, probably from one of the floorboards. A light shone through the crack under the door. I tried to slide back down as quickly as I could. If he found me on the steps there was no telling what he would do.

The door in the middle of the far wall is the other entrance to the basement. I head toward it, scanning the room as I walk across it. I run my hand across my forehead and realize I'm sweating even though I feel cold. I drop to my knees to check underneath the sofa, but there's nothing there. I stand back up and take a deep breath. There's some sort of folded metal thing on the floor next to the sofa. Two long tubes are leaning against it. I tuck my hair behind my ears and shuffle forward.

There is a low bench right by the set of weights. The blankets on the floor nearest the weights are piled in an odd fashion. I squint at them, then gasp as I see a foot sticking out.

Those aren't blankets. It's Ashley!

I shuffled backwards, sniffling back tears, my knees banging as I moved as fast as I could down the stone steps. He's supposed to be asleep! Why isn't he asleep? The door swung open before I made it all the way down. He stood there silhouetted by the light behind him. I tried to crouch down, hoping against all logic that he wouldn't see me, that he would just go away.

Even that far away he reeked of whiskey. "I have a surprise for you," he announced, his tone mocking. He was holding something in his hand, his fingers clenched tight around it. I blinked, trying to focus on what it was.

I freeze, staring at the body of my friend. I feel *déjà vu* so strong I want to retch.

I shuffle slowly toward her, afraid to look more closely, afraid to find out what horrible things were done to her. When I'm almost to her body I bump into the old wall. I press my hands flat against my invisible barricade, rubbing them over the surface, feeling the texture of each stone in the nonexistent wall, searching for a way through. There is none, of course. I'm so close I could touch her if it weren't for my wall, but I can't reach her. Not that I could do anything if I were able to get closer. She's dead. There's nothing to be done.

I slide to my knees and press my face against the wall that isn't there. Oh, poor Ashley. Her face is bruised and puffy, and one eye is swollen shut. Her long brown hair is splayed out like a fan, except for one section on the side of her head that's matted with dried blood. She's curled up into a little ball partly covered by an old, worn blanket. Her legs are wrapped around the metal pole of an old barbell, and her ankles are tied together with something small and white. Her wrists are bound with thick, gray tape. The weights on the barbell are very large, and look awfully heavy. She's wearing the same outfit her ghost self wore when we first met, although her blouse is ripped, one sneaker is missing, and her top and her jeans are stained with blood. She must have lost an awful lot of blood. Several of the buttons on her blouse are missing, and the top button is fastened to the wrong buttonhole.

This is almost like watching yet another horror movie, but this is Ashley, a real person — my friend — not some actor pretending to be dead.

Both of us murdered in the same place. What a bond to share with your friend.

I stare at her for a while, ghostly tears trickling down my face, then falling off my cheeks and turning into nothingness.

I stood there after he killed me. I was empty. Lost. The only sound I could hear was his laughter. Then he took a step backward and touched me. It was as if I'd been stabbed through with a million spears, like I'd been set on fire while alive. He was thinking about me, about how happy he was to have killed me. For that brief moment I was him, and I — he — was truly happy. That's when I realized why he'd looked so familiar, because being him I knew who he was. Luther Wallace Curdy, although of course I didn't know his name until I read his mind.

I'd only seen him once before, when I was eleven. I'd gone to the general store with Mama. She was looking at the new calicos, and I wandered outside to look at the horses. I stood there admiring a beautiful bay that was tied up at the rail, then I saw him. He was leaning against the building, grinning, staring at me with those pale eyes. I shivered and ran back inside.

Now I knew him — I was him. He'd remembered me all these years. He went off to the mines, and one day murdered a woman. He enjoyed killing her, so he killed another woman, and another. Then he'd come down from the mountains looking for me. Looking for me! After all those years he still remembered me.

Finally he stepped away, and out of me, after far too long. I stood there, my mind full of his thoughts, my eyes glued to my body. I was too confused by my death — and by becoming him — to understand anything. Nothing made sense, nothing at all.

I shuffled away from him toward the steps, then turned back to look at myself. My body lay sprawled on the floor, the rope pulled tight around my neck. My face was an awful purplish-red, and my eyes bugged out. It didn't look like me, not anymore. It wasn't me. Anymore.

He kicked my lifeless body with a heavy, booted foot. "Bitch! I got you good, now!" I felt blank, emotionless, as I watched him kick me over and over. With each kick of his leg my body moved a bit, my limp arms flopping about. He stopped, panting, for a moment, then nudged my corpse with his foot until my body was lying on its back, legs splayed wide. He chuckled and began to unbutton his trousers.

I turned away and walked up the stairs, unbound. Unscathed. Dead.

A creak from one of the floorboards above my head reminds me where I am, and I shudder. I should go see if Ashley has come back so I can let her know she's no longer missing, or at least is only missing to the living.

How am I going to tell her I've found her body? She'll probably want to come down here and see it, and then she'll have that memory, like I have mine. Maybe I shouldn't tell her. But that doesn't feel right at all. She deserves to know. Besides, sooner or later she'd come down here, or else someone will come down here and find it. Eventually someone will find it. Although no one has been here for years, except Ashley and her murderer, so it could be a while. But it must already be decomposing, and — I grimace — it will probably smell awful soon, so they'll notice it from upstairs. And poor Ashley will have to see herself half rotted.

I poke angrily at the floor.

I reached the main floor and went straight to the front door, the one he'd brought me through. I stepped out on the porch. The sun was shining, and the sky was a beautiful bright blue, empty of clouds. To my right I could see the mountains, the brown peaks of the foothills contrasting with the snowcaps of the higher mountains behind them. I wasn't thinking of anything much. I just wanted to leave. Now that I was able. I walked down the wooden stairs, and on the bottom step I lifted my leg up — then my knee smacked into an invisible barrier. Perplexed, I tried again. And again. I couldn't go any further. I walked around the porch and tried everything I could think of — climbing on the railing, then leaping off; flinging myself over the railing along the stairs; climbing the posts holding up the roof. No matter what

I tried I could not leave. I ran around the house, trying every window, trying the back door. Nothing worked.

I must have spent the next few days on the second floor, staring out at the mountains, my mind as empty as the cloudless sky. I didn't want to do anything else. I didn't try to leave the house again. I just sat on the pine floor, in an empty room, alone.

When I finally went down to the main floor, he was gone. The ashes in the fireplace were cold, his things were missing, and all the doors were wide open. I peered through the entrance to the cellar. From the doorway I could see the steps leading down into the darkness, and a small section of the dirt floor. I walked down the steps, my footsteps slow and timid. I could feel my heart beating hard in my chest, but I knew I was dead, and my heart wasn't real, couldn't be real. If I was dead, he couldn't hurt me. Right? I stopped halfway down the stairs, looking at the place where I'd been kept prisoner, tied up and treated like an animal. The place where I was murdered.

The only thing left was a pile of dirty straw.

I sigh and stand up, then turn and start back the way I came.

There's a small *swoosh* behind me and I whip around, but no one is there — only Ashley's broken body lying on the floor. I stand still, but hear nothing else. The noise must have come from outside. Prickles run down my back as I realize it could be Edward, coming back to take her body away. Maybe he won't leave her down here after all.

I wait for several minutes, then decide it was just a sound from outside. I start back the way I came, then turn around as I hear the noise again. My eyes dart around the room, then settle on Ashley's body as I realize what I heard.

Ashley is breathing.

Nine

Ashley is alive! She's not a ghost — she's alive! A roaring sound fills my ears as I stare at her.

If she's alive, how can she not be in her own body? I left mine when I died — not before. But the Ashley I know most certainly isn't a living person. Her soul, or her spirit, or whatever makes us alive, must have left her body. That's why I thought she was a ghost — and that's why she doesn't follow the same rules as me! But why did she leave her body in the first place? *How* did she leave it?

I gnaw on my knuckles. I can't believe she's not a ghost — I can't believe it!

But there she is, lying right in front of me. Physically, at least.

This makes no sense.

Her breath is ragged and slow. The blood on the side of her head has left dried trails down her cheek, and her face is terribly pale in the little bit of light that's fighting its way through the two tiny, filthy windows.

Perhaps she is almost dead? That happens sometimes in movies. I've seen films where a person having surgery almost dies and their spirit leaves their body, then comes back when they're alive again. But wait — in movies they are always *dead*. Not for very long, but someone's spirit can only be out of their body when they are completely dead. Ashley is clearly breathing. Could she have been down here for the past few days, repeatedly dying and then coming back to life? That's just not possible. I've spent hours with her at a stretch. If a person is dead for too long they are dead forever.

Maybe she is unconscious and her spirit wandered off. I guess that might be possible, although if that kind of thing happened all the time there should be an awful lot of spirits flitting about.

I bite too hard on a knuckle and jerk it out of my mouth, muffling my exclamation even though I know Ashley can't hear me. Or at least Ashley's body can't hear me. Or can she? I don't understand this, I don't understand it at all!

The raspy sound of her breathing is so soft it's almost unnoticeable. If I hadn't heard it I would have gone upstairs and told Ashley she is dead, but she's not. Not quite. I twist around and peer at her from different angles, unable to get very close because of my invisible wall, but I can't determine if she's unconscious or sleeping. I probably wouldn't be able to tell the difference even if I could get closer.

I rub my eyes, then run my fingers through my hair. I've never heard of anything like this happening. But there she is.

How am I going to tell Ashley she's still alive?

Edward did this to her. I don't know why, but then I still don't understand why my murderer did what he did, other than the fact that he was an evil, evil man. Edward must know she's not dead. What if he comes back to kill her? I stare at her, the hair standing up on the back of my neck. She has to come down here — she has to get back in her body, and escape! Has she forgotten where it is? Is that why she's wandering around? Is that why she doesn't remember what happened?

My knees feel weak. I have to help her. I have to get Ashley back in her body. That's where she belongs. That's where she should be. She could escape — she could get away before Edward murders her I can't let her be killed.

I turn around and run as fast as I can on my wobbly legs. I stumble out into the hall and sprint up the stairs, passing through the basement door, and plow straight into Jeremy Smithers —

... that blonde chick at the counter is hot ... look at that rack! ... good thing Marge can't read my thoughts or she'd have my —

I'm moving so rapidly that I'm through Jeremy in a split second, then I barrel right into Marge —

... that bastard ... he doesn't think I can tell he's staring at that little tramp ... I'll sneak some mangoes into dessert tonight and he'll wake up tomorrow with a rash ... I'll call Mother, too, and have her —

I'm in and out of the pair before I can stop myself. I stop next to the closest rack of movies, my hands grasping at the shelves as I try to catch my balance. I stand there wide-eyed, soiled by the couple's personalities. My desperate need to find

Ashley has been submerged, for the moment, by the need to pull myself free, to be me again. What a mean couple — they deserve each other. I shudder and look around the room. The store is awfully crowded. Of course — it's Friday night.

"Ashley? Are you here?"

… mangoes taste kind of like pine trees, like the way pine trees smell … I love eating them …

… I hate mangoes … such a nasty, squishy fruit. They give me a terrible rash, itchy as hell, and it lasts for a week …

… I sneak them into desserts sometimes just to spite Jeremy …

… she doesn't have any idea that I got a bonus at work. I'm going to buy —

I shake my head so furiously my hair ends up in a tangle in front of my eyes. I've never even seen a mango, much less eaten one. Leftover bits of Marge and Jeremy float in my mind, twisting around each other, clouding my identity. I don't have time for this. I don't know how much longer it will be before Edward returns to kill Ashley.

I pull my hair out of my face, then shrink back, pressing myself against the rack, as a large woman approaches me on my left and a chubby little boy runs toward her from my right, waving his arms and yelling. No, oh please no. I can't bear to touch another person right now.

The boy plows straight toward me. He's about to run right through me, so I back *into* the shelves to avoid being touched again. I turn around and peek into the next aisle, my body still inside the wooden shelves and the movie cases. There's no one on that side, although there are people at either end of the row, so I ooze through.

"Ashley!" I yell. My voice sounds hollow, fake — it doesn't carry, it doesn't echo. *Where is she?*

I step on the bottom shelf and clamber up until I can see over the rack. I scan the room, but don't see her —

There's a pale green sweater by one of the front windows. I leap down and run toward the window, frantically dodging customers along the way.

"Ashley!"

The girl in the sweater turns her head, revealing a large, slightly crooked nose. She's not Ashley.

I skid to a stop, then lean my back against the window and slide down until I'm sitting on the windowsill. I stare at my sneakered feet. They look foreign, unfamiliar, even though I've been wearing these newfangled shoes for ages.

"Hey, Emma. What's going on?"

I jerk my head up to see Ashley standing right in front of me. I start to reach out to her, then catch my breath and stop, my arms still stretched out in front of me.

She's sporting a hot pink tank top, a tight pink and white-checkered mini-skirt, and ridiculously high-heeled white pumps. Her long hair is pulled back in a ponytail, and her lipstick sparkles. She's wearing false eyelashes and has doused her eyelids in pink glitter.

I have no idea what to make of this transformation.

She grins, and blows a large pink bubble. My hands float slowly down to my sides.

"What do you think?" She turns from side to side to show off her outfit. The chubby boy meanders through Ashley; she doesn't even notice.

I open my mouth, then close it again, my life-saving mission momentarily derailed.

"I love this clothes-changing thing! It's really pretty easy. You just need to concentrate." She blows another bubble, which bursts with a loud pop.

"We should work on you. Have you ever worn make-up? Did it even exist when you were alive?"

"Wh — wh —" I stutter, then freeze as someone bumps into my shoulder —

… I should rent a funny movie … no… no, a scary movie … no … well, maybe —

I spring up off the windowsill. Meredith Johnson is standing next to me, scratching the dry, and rather itchy, skin showing through her thinning blonde hair. She rents a movie every Friday, and bowls every Monday, and loves artichokes on pizza. I shudder, feeling the part of Meredith that has momentarily become a part of me. My guard is not just down, it's nonexistent. I've touched *three* people in one night.

I edge further away from Meredith, trying to focus on Ashley while keeping one eye on Meredith. I grit my teeth as I resist the urge to scratch my head.

"I found —"

How do you tell someone you've found their body?

"You. Uh."

I rub my shoulder. The spot Meredith touched feels dirty, as though it was covered in mud. I attempt to compose myself.

"I found something really important."

… I can totally imagine that girl topless, on a trampoline … maybe a scary movie … her tits are huge … while he's asleep I'll

snip off little chunks of his hair ... I can't forget to buy that deep pore cleansing lotion ... she must have huge nipples, too ... I think I'm getting another zit ... it'll take him days to notice his hair ...

I put my hand out to the wall to keep from falling over and blink several times, trying desperately to stay focused on Ashley.

Ashley holds up her hand to admire her pink nails, which match her outfit perfectly. "This is so awesome. I love being a ghost!" She attempts a pirouette, barely catching herself as her high heels cause her to lose her balance.

I have to tell her, I have to get her to do something or she really will be a ghost! I have a flash of our future together if she dies. We'll haunt the store together, changing our hairstyles and outfits several times a day.

But we'll always be color coordinated.

"Ashley, I have to — I found — I mean —"

I'm babbling. I feel dizzy, as if I might collapse. Which is ridiculous. I'm dead — I'm certainly not going to faint.

I open my mouth, ready to tell her about my discovery.

"You're — you're sparkly."

I snap my mouth closed, shocked by what just came out of it. The girl is barely holding on to life, and *that's* what I say?

I stare at her, perplexed by my own behavior.

"Don't you just love the glitter?" Ashley beams. "I don't know what made me think of it. It's kind of retro, you know, but I thought I'd try it out."

She narrows her eyes as she looks at me. "Have you ever worn eyeliner? I think maybe brown — no, purple."

My heart is beating madly away. What's wrong with me? Why am I not telling her? Every second counts.

"I — n — no —" I stammer.

I have to tell her, I have to — if she can get back into her body she can escape. She won't be stuck here, she won't be a ghost.

Like I am.

Realizing the source of my reticence is like being hit with a bucket of ice-cold water.

Ashley babbles on, oblivious to my revelation.

"You have to be kidding me. What did girls do back in the 1800s? Nothing?" She rolls her eyes. "You totally need me to help you. I don't know how you managed without me."

I want to wrap my arms around her, I want to hug her. My one and only friend. I want her to stay.

I want her to be a real ghost, so she'll be stuck here, like me. With me.

I want her to stay.

I want her to die.

Ashley twirls around, clumsy in her heels.

"These might be a little too high," she grumbles, glaring at her shoes. "Aren't we supposed to be able to fly or float or something? Who made up these rules? Like, why do I have to deal with gravity if I'm dead?"

But you're not dead.

Yet.

I turn my head and stare down the aisle, away from her.

"The rules don't make any sense." I mutter. "They're stupid."

Why did I have to find Ashley's body? Why couldn't Edward have taken her somewhere else?

She exhales suddenly, the burst of air sounding like a steam engine's whistle.

"At least there are plenty of people to watch. I mean, it kind of sucks being dead, but there's all kinds of things to do."

But there aren't. Watching people live isn't the same as *living*.

I've been so alone. I hadn't realized just how awful loneliness was until Ashley arrived.

"Ashley, I —"

My tongue feels like it's twice its normal size. I close my eyes for a few seconds and take a deep breath. When I open my eyes I see Ashley scowling at something to my right.

"Did you see that guy over there? He bumped into that woman and then apologized, but I think he did it on purpose so he could touch her butt. What an asshole."

I'm stuck here. I'll be stuck here forever. Someday this house too will burn to the ground, or be torn down. Maybe there will be an earthquake, or another ice age, and there won't be any people left for me to watch.

I picture the planet colder, all civilization gone, humanity extinct or living in caves and barely surviving. And I'll be here, haunting the house of my murder even though it'll be just a spot of barren, windswept, snow-covered land.

"Ashley, I found you." I hear myself say. "You're not dead."

The wind howls in my mind, blowing snow across my tiny world.

Her expression is blank. "What are you talking about? I'm *missing*. I went back home today, and they still haven't found my body. But I'm dead all right. Haven't you noticed?"

She raises an eyebrow as she jams her forefinger through the wall.

"See? Seems pretty obvious to me."

137

She blinks several times, the fake lashes fluttering like miniature black feathers.

But she's *not* a ghost. She's alive, and she's going to stay alive.

"You aren't dead," I insist, my voice firm. "Not yet. But have to go back to your body soon, or you really will die."

I step backward as Meredith shuffles past, her sensible brown shoes sliding along the worn carpet. From her expression I can tell that she still hasn't made a decision. I have a sudden craving for artichoke pizza.

Ashley stares at me, expressionless.

"Your body is downstairs, but you're unconscious, not a ghost. You have to go back to it and wake up, then you can escape!" I grab her shoulder. "Ashley, you're alive!"

"Whatever," Ashley snaps. She shrugs off my hand, then turns and sashays toward the front of the store, her hips swaying in their checkered encasing. She wobbles and almost falls, but catches herself on the edge of a shelf.

"Don't you understand? You're *alive!*" I yell. She ignores me and keeps going. I stand there with my mouth open and watch as Ashley walks through people, and they walk through her. It doesn't affect her at all.

That'll change if she truly becomes a ghost.

A lot of things will change.

I now know why Ashley can leave the store, and why she isn't affected when she touches people. When she dies she'll haunt the store — but the current store, not *my* building. We'll overlap in most areas, but she won't be able to get to the sidewalk that wraps around the building, in between the store and the card shop next door. She'll be able to go to the west side of the building, where the kitchen used to be, and I won't be able to follow her. I can see the two of us fifty years from now — her in that ridiculous checkered miniskirt, me in plain blue jeans, each sulking in the one area the other person can't go.

Eventually I'll even try wearing false eyelashes.

Why didn't she want to listen to me? She should have been excited that I found her body — and especially that she's not dead. It was as if she didn't believe me at all.

Or that she didn't *want* to believe me.

If I'd left my body after I'd been assaulted and someone told me I was still alive, would I have wanted to go back to it? *Could* I have gone back? And what can Ashley possibly do if her spirit re-enters her body, if such a thing is even possible? She's attached to a barbell and seriously injured — she's not going to be able to go anywhere!

It would be like me choosing to return to being tied up in the cellar. Going back to being naked, shivering in the ever-present cold, with my bruises and broken wrist.

Back to knowing that *he* was upstairs, plotting new ways to hurt me, to humiliate me.

Back to knowing there was no escape.

Pretending that I was dead might have been easier than admitting the truth.

He slapped my face so hard that I fell over. I landed on my shoulder, then sprawled across the pile of straw, pieces of it digging into the raw skin on my scraped cheek. I hid my face in my hands as he kicked me in the stomach. With each kick the rope binding my wrists dug into my chin. A sharp pain pierced my middle. I gasped, my breaths quick and shallow — I couldn't breathe right,

I couldn't get enough air! He stopped kicking and laughed, a long, harsh laugh, As he put his hand on his belt I closed my eyes tight.

I don't know how Ashley left her body — and maybe she doesn't either.

But I know why.

There are fewer people around now, but instead of wending my way through them I observe Ashley from across the room. She's perched on the end of the counter nearest the computer, swinging her feet back and forth and blowing large, pink bubbles while she observes the customers.

Is she pretending nothing happened? Or has she allowed herself to forget it all? Is it really possible to do something, then convince yourself that it never happened?

I've seen plenty of movies in which people do just that.

An old man wearing a brown and red plaid shirt comes up to the counter to pay for his movie, and Ashley sticks her tongue out at him. I can't tell if she knows him or if she's just entertaining herself.

I don't know how to convince her I'm telling the truth. She doesn't want to believe me. In an awful way it's easier to avoid facing reality, even if it means letting yourself die.

The clock strikes eleven.

The store closes in an hour. Edward will probably wait until everyone is gone, and then come back to finish what he started.

I push myself off of the wall and head over toward the counter where Ashley is sitting. She's still blowing bubbles, apparently oblivious to the fact that she is dying.

I don't know what to say, but I have to say something. Somehow I have to convince her to listen to me. Maybe I can explain how her life, or more correctly, her death, will change things. She's got to go back to her body and at least *try* to escape. I don't know how she can, but Edward seems to have left her in the basement, alone, so maybe there's a way. Maybe.

I wish I knew if the other door to the basement was locked. It's past my boundaries, so there's no way for me to know.

Edward would be foolish to have left it unlocked.

If I were a ghost in a movie I bet I'd be able to open it.

Ashley is slouching with her back against the wall. Her knees are bent and her bare feet rest on the counter, the high-heeled shoes gone. The polish on her toenails matches her fingernails. She's wearing a lovely knitted shawl, done in a soft white yarn that contains silver sparkles. I don't know how she thought that up. She's probably never knitted anything in her life.

"Emma!" she exclaims warmly. "I've been having *such* a great time!"

She slides her feet off the counter and pats a spot next to her.

I hoist myself onto the counter next to Ashley.

"I'm glad it's been fun." My voice sounds hollow, as if I'm attempting to sound cheery at a funeral. "It's Friday, so there's more of a bustle than normal."

There's a harsh sound behind me and I jerk around, but it was just an old man clearing his throat.

"Saturdays are usually busy, too," I blurt. I sound ridiculous.

Ashley giggles, oblivious to my plight.

"Don't these people know they can watch movies any night of the week?" She sneers at an elderly woman on the other side of the room. "They don't have to wait for the weekend. Idiots."

"Ashley, you have to go back." I twist my fingers together, willing her to listen, to believe.

She sighs and rolls her eyes. "You're not starting on *that* again, are you? Jesus, Emma."

"I know you're afraid, but you're not dead. You can go back, you can escape, and live! You have to live!"

"I'm a fucking *ghost*, Emma. Would you knock it off and let me start enjoying myself?" She crosses her arms and glowers at the movie playing on the screen across from the counter.

This is not going well at all.

Perhaps if I show Ashley some of the negatives of being a ghost, she might be willing to listen to me and return to her body? She'll find a way to rip the tape off her wrists, then she'll break open the locked door and run off to safety in spite of her weakened state.

It'll be easy. Just like in the movies.

I close my eyes. I don't know if there's any way this could possibly work. But she's got to try. She's got to. I can't let her die.

If only superheroes were as real as ghosts are.

I open my eyes and plow forward with plan B. I'm not exactly sure what it entails, but I'm going to convince her no matter what it takes.

"Too bad they aren't showing a good film tonight." I gesture toward the screen.

"Oh, no, this one is great!" Ashley shakes her head. "I've only seen it three times so far." She tugs on the hem of her skirt. It's awfully short, so it doesn't much matter if she pulls it down an eighth of an inch.

"Well, I must say," I force a deep sigh. "After you see a film a few hundred times it becomes a bit boring."

She looks at me sharply. "Didn't this movie just show up in the store yesterday? That's what the helper girl —" She waves vaguely around, "said to one of the customers."

Darn it — why couldn't the movie playing now be one she's watched over and over? I attempt to keep my face expressionless. I was always a terrible liar, but hopefully Ashley won't be able to see through me like Lizzie used to.

"That's right, but sometimes movies show up at the store before they're allowed to rent them out."

I can hear the dishonesty in my voice. Fortunately Ashley doesn't.

"Really? That's cool!"

This approach is clearly not working. I glance at her out of the corner of my eye.

"Not as cool as going to see a movie in a theater," I sigh longingly. "I've never been to a real movie theater."

"What? Oh, right, because you're stuck haunting this store." She nods and turns back to the television screen.

I'm trying to save her life, and she's making light of my situation. It would serve her right to die and be stuck here, too. But she doesn't understand — and if she's lucky, she never will.

"Well, in a manner of speaking." I have to convince her being a ghost isn't always fun — and this might just do it. "I haunt the house I was killed in. But it's not the same as the building we're in now."

"Yeah, you said something about another house before." She stops watching the movie and looks at me, her eyes filled with curiosity. It's about time I got her attention.

"The house I died in looked like this." I make a roughly rectangular shape with my hands.

"But then it burned down."

Lightning struck the roof one wild night; a bolt of electricity thrust through the roof of the house, through each floor, burning holes in everything it touched. I was curled up in a corner in the front room. It came through the ceiling and plunged straight down into the cellar. The fire started on the second story, weak at first, but growing bigger and stronger until the house filled with smoke that would have choked a living person. The blaze was fierce and determined, the red-gold flames sweeping through the house, sweeping through me. And then everything was gone.

"Years later this house was built."

I move my hands apart, exaggerating the size of the new house. I should tell her what it's like to haunt nothing, to haunt a house when none exists. How it feels to bang your fists against a wall that isn't there, to feel its texture underneath your fingers while you can see its ashes smoldering at your feet. I should tell her what it's like to spend years without a roof overhead, having the wind howl right through you, watching raindrops fall through your body to land on the ground.

It was a long, long time before the second house was erected.

"I haunt the house that I was killed in, even though it is smaller than the building we're in, and I can't leave it. Which means that I can't get to parts of the store that didn't exist when I died."

I point at the counter that stands between us and the room that used to be the kitchen.

"For example, I can't go into the back room at all."

"Wow, that sucks!" Her face is filled with a simple sympathy, as if she were consoling a friend who'd lost an earring.

This isn't working either.

What might she understand? What can I say? I can't just leap back into the topic of her body. But she's got to go back to it, and soon. I can feel it in my bones, even if they don't exist. I have to convince her. I can't let her die.

"So let's say that someday this store burns down."

She shakes her head. "The firemen won't let that happen. They're only a block over."

"Uh. Good point. But what if someday, say a hundred years in the future, when there are flying cars —" She looks excited. Great!

"And they build a mall right here, right where this house is now, and it has lots of little shops — clothing shops, shoe shops, um —" She's totally focused.

"Shops with cute things."

She nods happily.

"And you can't walk around the mall because you're stuck haunting the house you died in."

"That isn't fair! Besides, that house won't be there anymore. And who cares about a mall? How shallow do you think I am?" She fiddles with the end of her ponytail, her nails shiny and bright with color.

"But that's how it works for me, so once you're truly dead that's how it will work for you."

I try to keep my voice soft and empathetic, even though I want to yell: *No, it isn't fair!*

"It's a rule of being a ghost — you haunt where you died." I don't really know that it's a rule — it's a rule for *me*, certainly.

145

What if she has different rules as a ghost, just like she has different rules now? My chest tightens.

"For real?" She scowls.

"For real." I press my lips together. Enough of this approach. Time is ticking away while I try to tiptoe around her stubbornness.

"That's why you *have* to listen to me, even though I know you don't want to."

She looks away.

If Lizzie had died … The back of my neck feels all prickly.

"Ashley, listen!" My voice is firm. "You *aren't dead*! You aren't trapped here, like me — you can still escape!"

She stares at the wall across from us. There's a whiteboard hanging there, listing which movies will be released on which day, but she's not looking at it. Her lips move, but she doesn't say anything.

"Ashley, you have a chance to save yourself, to be *alive*! You've got to go back to your body and at least try to escape, or you will never forgive yourself!"

I will never forgive *myself* if she doesn't try. I can't drag her to the basement and stuff her back into her body. But I need her to try! I need her to escape! Somehow …

I feel inexplicably guilty.

The bell on the front door jangles softly, and Savannah enters.

She's wearing the same outfit she had on earlier today, with the addition of a puffy down jacket. At least it's not lavender like the rest of her outfit — it's a soft powder blue. She heads directly to the bulletin board across from the stairs, and stands there inspecting the postings.

"Isn't that your friend?" I whisper, although I know exactly who it is. In some ways I know Savannah better than Ashley does.

"Yeah," she whispers back. "What is she doing?"

We watch as Savannah stares at the various postings on the bulletin board, then reaches behind a bright purple piece of paper. She tugs for a second, then her fingers reappear, holding a small, white square. It looks like a piece of notebook paper all folded up. Savannah squirrels the square away in her jacket pocket and walks out the door, a satisfied smile on her face.

"What is going on?" Ashley demands. "Can't you read her mind?"

"Only if I touch her." I say dryly.

Matt probably left the note for her, arranging to meet her, although I can't fathom why he'd be so sneaky. Maybe because she's so young. My stomach churns. Savannah is awfully young to get involved with a man Matt's age, especially in this time. How old is he anyway? Maybe twenty–five? And Savannah is Lizzie's age! I'm torn between jealousy and indignation.

"I bet she got a date with Dane," Ashley announces.

Who?

"Dane?"

"His name's really Dan, but he's Danish, or part-Danish, or something." Ashley jumps to the floor.

"So we call him that. Anyway, he's really cute. I bet he left a secret note here for Savannah. And she didn't even tell me!"

"If she thinks you're dead, which you are *not*, she can't very well tell you who she's dating," I snap.

"Missing! I'm *missing*, not dead!" Ashley insists. "At least —" she pauses. "I'm not dead *yet*." She walks away from me, toward the bulletin board.

"I mean, they don't know for sure I'm dead yet. But I am."
She sounds smaller, less sure of herself. She glances toward the
front window.

There's one more thing I could try. It's harsh, but maybe
that's what it will take to convince her to listen to me. And for
all I know it could be true.

"Ashley, what if the guy who captured you goes after
Savannah next?" Her back stiffens.

"I know you know you're not dead — but you will be if
you don't try to escape. And if you go back to your body you
could make sure no one else gets hurt by that man."

We stand there for a few minutes, the silence broken only
by the hum of the television.

Finally, Ashley whispers, "Do you think the note is from
her killer? From — "

Her voice drops so low I can barely make out the words.

"From *my* killer?"

I don't think that at all. I think the note is from Matt,
arranging a place to meet her.

"Yes," I lie. "I'm sure it is."

Ashley's eyes are fixed on the postings on the bulletin
board.

Nissan for sale, low miles!

Roommate needed, no cats, ferrets okay.

*Want to earn extra money? $12,000/month, part-time, and
you work from home!*

She's not reading them, though — she looks as though
she's somewhere far away. I clasp my hands together and stare
at the floor. There's a dark stain in the carpet right in front of

the counter. Years ago a little girl spilled grape soda there. For all I know that little girl was Ashley.

I stare at the discolored carpet. I wish I knew what to do. All I know is that I have to do *something*.

Ashley's voice trembles when she finally speaks.

"Will you go with me?"

Ten

Ashley is still staring in the direction of the bulletin board. Her face is pale and her mouth is a thin, tight, glitter-covered line.

"Of course I'll go with you."

I rest my hand on her shoulder. For a split second I have to fight the urge to jerk back, my reflexes stubborn after all these years of avoiding touch, then find I'm reluctant to pull it away. She feels so warm. So alive.

"I'll be with you the whole time, Ashley. I promise."

Not that I can do anything to help once she gets back in her body. Assuming she can even do that.

I go over to the door to the basement and stop just outside of it, then turn back toward her. She hasn't moved at all. Darn it all! I probably waited too long to talk to her the first time. If I have to convince her again from the beginning we might be too late to save her from dying for real.

We may already be too late.

Ashley pushes herself off the countertop and lands on the floor. She walks over to me, her movements slow and hesitant, her head hanging low. Her feet are still bare, the pink of her toenails almost garish in the harsh fluorescent light. She reaches me and stops. The angle of her head causes her hair to hang like a curtain across her face; it casts a shadow that makes her look even more somber. In the bright light I can see where her highlights are growing out. The roots are a deep, warm brown.

"It will be dark, but you'll be able to see."

At least I'm assuming she'll be able to see in the dark because she could last night. I hope there's not some rule that says unconscious people can only see when there's moonlight, or something ridiculous like that.

She stands there for a moment, staring at the floor, then nods.

I take a deep breath. I feel as though I'm leading her to her death, in spite of the fact that my goal is to keep her from dying. I steel myself, then take her cold, limp hand in mine, trying to tell myself that it's going to be okay, that somehow we'll figure out a way to save her. I used to hold Lizzie's hand just like this when we walked to school when we were little.

"Let's go."

I step through the door, then stop when I realize she isn't following me. Her wrist is on this side of the door, but her body hasn't moved. I tug on her disembodied hand. After a pause she walks through and joins me.

We huddle close together on the little landing and peer down into the stairwell. I can see the dirt floor far below us, and the stone wall on the right-hand side of the stairs. The earthy scent of my old prison mingles with that of the straw that served as my bedding.

I blink, and the wall of today overlays the stone wall from my past. The smell of damp earth is replaced by that of dust and age.

I want to run back into the safe familiarity of the store. I want to curl up on the checkered couch and hide my face, and pretend I never even found Ashley's body. But this is too big, too important. I don't want her to die!

I can't *let* her die.

Her fingers tighten around mine. They feel cold and fragile, as if they're made from bone china, like an old teacup.

"Emma?" Her voice is so faint I can hardly hear her. "Emma, I'm scared."

As am I.

I squeeze her hand, trying to will warmth and strength back into her. "I'm right here, Ashley."

I grab the railing with my left hand and take a step down. She follows me, mirroring my movements. Our shoulders are pressed close together, her grip on my hand so tight it hurts. The stairs seem to go on forever.

There's a soft, muffled jingle from upstairs as someone opens and closes the front door. It must be almost midnight. A lovely time to be doing something like this. On the other hand, since it's so late maybe that means Edward is less likely to show up. Or perhaps more likely …

I catch my breath and stumble. Ashley reaches out her arm to steady me. I hadn't thought about him showing up while Ashley tried to escape. What if he's down there right now? What if Ashley gets back in her body just in time for him to arrive and kill her?

"Are you okay?" Ashley breathes.

"Just lost my balance," I whisper back.

Why was Matt working this morning instead of Stacia? What if Stacia didn't show up because Edward kidnapped her? I try to remember if there was any mention about Stacia today, but I can't seem to recall a single thing anyone said. If Edward really did kidnap Stacia, they could be down there right now. I might have to try to save Ashley *and* Stacia.

Although — why did Edward come into the store today during the time that Stacia usually works? Oh, right. For an alibi. Murderers always have alibis in the movies. He can say he was in the store just like he usually is, and Stacia wasn't there, so he won't be a suspect at all. I'm the only one who noticed him tap the basement door when he left the store, and I certainly can't tell anyone. Except Ashley.

But, of course, Ashley already knows who he is.

Ashley's pace picks up slightly. She has a determined look that wasn't there a few minutes ago. Our hands are still clasped, but not as tightly as before. They —

Ashley vanishes.

My left foot misses the edge of the step and I lose my balance. I grab the railing with both hands, smack my head into the wall, and barely keep from plummeting down the stairs. What happened? Where did she go? She was *right here*!

We were holding hands — she disappeared while we were holding hands! My eyes dart about the empty stairwell. It remains empty. *Where is she?*

I suddenly realize where she must be.

I careen down the remaining stairs and into the room where her body lies. I skid to a stop right before I reach my wall and splay my hands on the invisible barrier, my heart thumping like mad.

A soft moan tells me I was right.

Ashley is conscious.

"Ashley!"

The bruises on her face seem slightly darker. The eye that isn't swollen shut flutters. She lifts her head, but doesn't look at me. It's as though she didn't even hear me.

I raise my voice.

"Ashley, it's Emma! I'm here!"

But she can't hear me. Not now.

Ashley squints around the room with her good eye. She's lying on her side and writhes about as if she wants to sit up, but then flops back down.

She's been here for two days now, is that right? No, three — I met her on Thursday, and she said she remembered being alive on Wednesday. That means she's been moving in and out of consciousness for *three days*. Has she had any food or water at all? How long is too long?

I beat my fists on the nonexistent wall. The stones that aren't there are hard and cold, firmly denying me access to my friend. Although there's nothing I could do if I could reach her.

Ashley tosses feebly, twisting around on the floor until she's so close to the barbell that her face is almost touching it. I think her left shoulder may be injured; she seems to be favoring it. It looks like she's trying to cut the duct tape binding her wrists on a nail head that's sticking out from the wall, but she can't lift her arms high enough to reach it.

I sit behind my barrier, a mere spectator.

Eventually she gives up her attempt and her arms fall to the ground, then she curls up into herself and lies still. She coughs, then makes a raspy, choking sound. Is she dying? Am I going to have to watch her die?

The choking turns into a sob, then the sob turns into a long, rattling breath. Her eyes close, and her breathing slows until I can't tell if she's even breathing anymore.

Is she dead? Please don't be dead, Ashley! Please!

I press my face against the invisible wall. No wait — she's still alive! I can see her chest rising and falling. The movement is slight, but it's there.

My jaw relaxes. I didn't even know I was clenching it. She's alive! But —

But she's still here, still a prisoner. I stare at my friend. I'm unable to even touch her, much less help her.

Ashley seems to move again, then splits in two as a second Ashley appears out of the first. I gape, not sure what is happening.

The first Ashley lies on the ground, one eye closed, the other swollen shut. The second Ashley props herself up on her elbow, both eyes open, healthy and whole. Her flowered blouse is the same as the one on the other Ashley, but hers is buttoned correctly, and free of blood. She glances down at her body, then sits up and looks directly at me. She's unbruised, unbattered.

This Ashley sees me.

We stare at each other for a moment. I realize my mouth is hanging open, and I snap it shut.

"I guess you were right after all," she says.

She brushes a strand of clean, unbloodied hair out of her face. Her torso, her spirit torso, is sitting up, but her hips and legs are taking up the exact same space as her physical body. It's a disconcerting image, as though she's two people with one set of legs.

"I didn't want to believe you. I didn't know it was all real. I truly didn't — I didn't remember anything." Her mouth droops, and her lower lip quivers slightly.

"But I do now. I remember everything. Now."

"I'm so sorry, Ashley." I thrust my hand out toward her and stub my thumb on my invisible barrier.

Ashley glances at her sad double, supine on the floor, then pushes her spirit self up until she's standing. The contrast between her real and unreal bodies is shocking — the one hurt, beaten, devoid of life; the other bright, perky, glowing with energy. I feel a sense of relief as they separate and there are two Ashleys, instead of one strange conglomeration.

"Is this like what happened to you, Emma?"

I dreamed I was a little girl, walking to the schoolhouse with my friend Beverly. Lizzie was still too young to go, but not me. I was big! I would learn to read and write and everything! The sunshine was bright and warm on my shoulders, and Beverly and I skipped along, holding each other's hand. I sang a little tune that

Mama used to sing while she mended clothes. I didn't know all the words, so I made up nonsense words ...

A sharp clank from above sent my dream scurrying. I lay on my pile of straw, blinking, all the pain flooding back in a rush, the happiness and sunshine of my dream swept away by the unforgiving reality of my dark prison.

I heard his booted feet thumping on the floorboards. If only this was the dream. I struggled to a sitting position. A piece of my tattered dress got stuck under my foot, and I heard a loud rip as it tore.

"Close enough."

The ability of someone to be cruel, to inflict pain on another human being, isn't unique to my time, nor to Ashley's.

She walks over and stands next to me. I put my arm around her shoulders and we stare at her body.

It's so small and sad, curled up on itself. It looks like Ashley — it *is* Ashley. But at the same time it's almost as if it's someone else, the sorrow and pain on its face unlike anything of the Ashley I know.

"I can't escape," she announces, her tone matter-of-fact.

"Yes, you can," I insist. But what if she's right? My heart thumps so loud it's a wonder Ashley can't hear it too.

She shakes her head, her face solemn.

"I tried to get the tape off, but I couldn't. I can't move my arms very well, so they won't lift up high enough." She rubs her left shoulder. "And I don't have any idea what to do about my feet."

Now that her body is at a different angle I can see that her feet are bound with a thin, white band of plastic.

"That's a zip tie," she explains. "It's pretty much impossible to get out of unless you have scissors or something. The police use them all the time these days."

The rope around my ankles was tight, the knot drawn so fast I couldn't get it to budge. If it wasn't there I would have been able to walk up the stairs. He told me the door wasn't locked — he told me! Sneering at me, as if it was a challenge — as if I could escape, if I only tried hard enough. But I couldn't stand up the way he'd tied me. I tried, but I couldn't. All I could do was crawl. And I was so tired; it had been days and days... I was just so tired.

"We have to do something," I mutter, scowling at the barbell. "There has to be some way to get you out of here."

"I know you want me to escape, but I *can't*. I'm tied up, and — it's just ridiculous." She throws her hands up in the air. "I can't get that stupid duct tape off my wrists. I tried, I tried so hard! I kept trying to reach that nail — " she points to the nail sticking out of the wall. "But I couldn't. I can't seem to bend the right way. There's something wrong with my shoulder and it just won't move enough to let me reach, and I really tried even though it hurts like hell. And even if I could get my hands free, what could I possibly do then? All the crap in this stupid room, and I can't see anything that might cut that fucking zip tie!"

I don't point out that the door might be locked as well.

"I give up. I'm done. I'm not going to bother anymore. I don't want to be a ghost. I don't want to be dead! But it *hurts* to be in my body. It hurts so much! I'm not going back. There's no point. Besides —"

She takes a few steps away from herself.

"Besides, I don't want to have those awful memories. Maybe I can just forget them." She nods firmly, as though she's made a decision. "I didn't remember I was here until you reminded me. I can forget it all again. I'm sure I can."

You can't forget things like that. You can lie to yourself, you can pretend that they never happened — but your mind will file it all away somewhere. Whether she lives or dies, she's going to have all the memories she doesn't want. The memory of the abduction, of the pain, of trying — and failing — to escape.

"Ashley, you're not going to forget. You just can't hide that sort of thing from yourself. I'm sorry."

I wish she could. I wish *I* could.

She glares at me, her eyes narrowed.

"Well, I'm going to try really hard!"

We stand there in silence for a few minutes. Finally she sighs.

"I'm sorry. I'm so scared, and it hurts *so* much. And I just passed out, so there's nothing I can do until I wake up again." She runs her fingers through her hair.

"My, uh, my body is worn out. It needs to rest for a little while. I — it — haven't, or uh, hasn't had anything to eat or drink for days. Maybe — " She rubs her forehead.

"Could you ... can you help me think about what to do the next time I wake up?"

Her eyes plead with me, and her face shines with hope. What can I possibly suggest she do?

"Of course. I'll think of something." My voice is firm, sure, as if it's just a matter of time before I craft the perfect escape plan.

Ashley can't see the lump I feel in my throat.

I scan the room, searching for anything that might help.

Ashley's body is lying under the corner of an old, tattered blanket near an old shoebox and a pile of magazines. The barbell her legs are attached to is sitting next to a neat stack of round weights. The largest weights are on the barbell, so presumably they're the heaviest. There's a low bench nearby, and a pair of thick black gloves lie on the floor next to the bench. They look exactly like the gloves Edward was wearing the other day.

There are some boxes and a small refrigerator on the south wall by the bed. The refrigerator wasn't here the last time I walked my boundaries. There are two lamps by the sofa and a laptop computer lying on the floor, with something black next to it that looks like a camera. A shelf by the bed holds some cardboard packages that might contain food, although I can't tell for sure from this distance.

"Do you remember anything special about the — your — the guy who kidnapped you? Anything that might help us?" I caught myself before I called him her murderer. He's not that yet, at least.

"I, um." She blinks rapidly. "I — he, um. Hmmm." She pinches her lips together. "He — he grabbed me when I was waiting for Savannah, and stuck me in the back of a van. A — a white van."

A van? Edward must have a motorcycle and a van. Ashley's face looks pained. "Then what?" I prompt.

She sighs and crinkles up her face.

"I know this is hard, Ashley, I really do. But you might remember something that could help."

"Well …" She turns her face to one side.

"He kept me in his van for a while. He hit me, and tied me up." Her eyes meet mine for a second, then she looks away.

"He's a horrible man. A very awful, evil —" Her voice breaks.

"I know," I say softly.

She takes a deep breath.

"Then he brought me here. It was late, really late at night. We came through that door," she points to the door on the west wall. The door I didn't remember was there. The door I wasn't watching.

"He carried me in. I was all tied up by that point." She sniffles. "Then he went away."

"Did he do anything else?" I can imagine what he did only too clearly.

"He ate some chips." She points at a crumpled plastic bag on the floor by the bed.

"He — ate chips."

"Yeah, they were garlic and jalapeño flavored. And then he drank a beer. That fridge is full of beer."

"Was he drunk?"

Maybe we can figure out a way to convince him to drink enough to get drunk, then she can overpower him? I don't know if that would work. Edward drunk would still be much stronger than Ashley — even if she wasn't in such a weakened state.

"Oh, no. He just had the one." She pauses and her eyes flit from side to side.

So much for that idea. I'm not sure how she could convince him to drink more anyway.

"What else happened?"

"He hit me. See?" She points to the side of her body's head.

"He smacked me there with a short piece of metal, like a pipe or something. I don't know what it was, but it hurt. I guess it must have knocked me out."

We both look around the room but there's nothing in sight that resembles a metal pipe.

"Then I don't remember anything until I met you."

She looks at me expectantly, as if I now have acquired enough information to save her.

"Okay. Let me think about this a little." I keep my voice sure and strong, like when Lizzie would have a nightmare, or when there was a noise outside our cabin. I'd tell her nothing bad would ever happen to her, to us.

"I just need to give this some thought, but I'll figure something out."

I glance at Ashley and force a smile. Sometimes I'd be scared in the middle of the night too, but I never let on to Lizzie.

My smile feels as though it's carved out of wood.

Eleven

We stand side by side and stare at Ashley's body, wretched in its bruised and bloody misery. The Ashley I've come to know is next to me — her hair clean and smooth, not matted with blood; her cheeks glowing with health, not mottled with bruises. But the other Ashley is the Ashley I know as well.

The spirit Ashley stomps her foot.

"There has to be *something* we can do!"

We stare at her body lying in a crumpled little pile on the floor, then she grabs my shoulder, her eyes wild.

"Have you ever tried to put a thought *in* a person's head? Like maybe you could make someone think about calling the police?"

My heart beats faster.

"No … no, I never have. Do you think I could?"

"I don't know!" She waves her hands in the air. "I have no idea! But what if you could?"

We turn as one and sprint across the room and up the stairs.

Can I do this? Have I truly never tried, even by accident?

We dash through the wooden door and slow to a stop next to the counter. Ashley is looking frantically at the people nearby. She points to a young girl walking by.

"What about her?"

The girl is Jenny Larkspur; I bumped into her a few years ago. Cotton candy wasn't even invented yet when I was alive, but thanks to her I now know exactly what it tastes like; how the sweet strands of sugar melt on your tongue, how you're left wanting more.

I wrinkle my nose at Jenny, a faint echo of sugar on my tongue.

"Do you think I should touch her and think about your body? Or about calling the police? If I just think about making a phone call that's probably not enough."

We stare at Jenny. She scratches her shoulder, oblivious to our scrutiny.

Ashley said her body needed to rest before she tried again. How long will it need? How long does she have? Edward might come back, eat some more garlic and jalapeño chips, and then kill her. And if not, how much longer can she survive without water?

"If you just think about calling them she might not do it because she won't know why she wants to make the call." Ashley points out. "So you should probably think about my body too."

"That makes sense." I take a deep breath, then reach out a shaking hand and enter Jenny's mind.

... This movie looks pretty good ... I should get gas on the way home ...

I picture Ashley, covered in blood, her legs bound.

... maybe I don't need to, though ... it's cold and I don't want to have to stand outside at the pump ...

I concentrate as hard as I can on the images: Ashley dying ... a telephone ... blood ... a police car ...

Jenny sees none of them.

... I wonder if there's any ice cream left? ... boy, that guy is cute ...

Through her eyes I recognize Matt's broad shoulders. Edward is standing a little ways behind Matt, lurking, waiting, watching Stacia, who he hasn't captured yet after all. Stacia's red fingernails flash brightly as her hands move back and forth, taking money, running credit cards, handing out movies. Edward is wearing his sunglasses even though the sun has gone down. Is he planning on abducting Stacia after the store closes? Or is he going to go downstairs and kill Ashley? Why does he have a second pair in the basement?

... I could stop and buy more ice cream just to be safe ...

I drag myself out of Jenny.

"It didn't work, Ashley, it didn't work at all — and he's *right there*! We have to go back downstairs and try again — now!"

"It didn't?" Her face is white. She turns toward Edward. "Omigod omigod, there he is!"

Edward moves to the next aisle and pretends to look at the movies on the shelf. Ashley stands as still as if she'd been frozen. I grab her arm.

"Come on, Ashley — we have to go!"

Ashley shakes herself, then dashes toward the basement door. I start to follow, then pause as I see Edward put a hand inside one of his coat pockets. What is he doing? Is it important? Should I wait and see?

Matt walks toward me. His eyes flicker across Jenny for the briefest of moments. Edward's hand is still in his pocket.

"Come on, Emma!" Ashley yells. I turn my head and look at her right as she moves through the door and is gone. I open my mouth to tell her I want to see what Edward is doing, just in case it helps us, somehow —

— and then Matt steps into me, touching me, his body overlapping my body, his mind in my mind.

… She's waiting outside in the car … everything is working out perfectly … tonight is the night. My night. The night I make my first — and second — kill … practice makes perfect … and you need to try different things until you find your true path in life … Dad was right … If only he knew what he'd inspired …

Matt grins, exposing his beautiful, straight, pearly teeth, his strong, muscular body overlapping mine. I feel him from the inside; his body and my body are one. Mine is faint, weak, pale — his is firm, powerful, real. I know now that the confidence he radiates is never forced; it's an intrinsic part of him. Matt has no doubts, no fears. And no compassion.

… Another fifteen minutes and I'm out of here … the van is ready and waiting, hidden in the bushes by the creek just outside of town … she won't suspect a thing until we're there, and there won't be anyone nearby to hear her …

The girl in the car is just a thing to him, but to me she's Savannah. I see her face in his memory; I smell the vanilla of her perfume. I feel excitement, expectation, satisfaction. These aren't *my* emotions — I don't want Matt to kidnap Savannah! I don't want him to murder her and Ashley!

I — Matt — *we* — picture the upcoming scene at the creek, the struggle when Savannah realizes what is happening and the pleasure we'll feel at overpowering her. We're stronger, and we're smarter. We enjoy this moment of anticipation as one small step in a night of pleasure, just like someone else might savor the tiniest lick of ice cream, prolonging the experience so that it lasts as long as possible.

... soon ... very soon ...

We touch Stacia lightly on the shoulder. Amazing how the tiniest bit of physical contact can do so much. Women are so predictable. And so pathetic. We could wring her neck like a wet rag, squeezing her life away right here in the store. But we won't. Yet.

"Stacia, I've been meaning to tell you all night that I love that eye shadow."

We hold her gaze just a little longer than she's comfortable with, but she likes it. They all do. We've practiced this endlessly; we know exactly how to use body language to manipulate women. Stacia looks flattered, and turns her eyes downward as if she's both pleased and embarrassed.

... works every fucking time ...

I see Stacia through Matt's eyes even though my own eyes are staring in a completely different direction. Mine see Edward, who has just pulled a set of keys out of his pocket. Matt's eyes watch Stacia, observing her reaction to his calculated charm. Edward glances down at his keys, then back at Stacia. His glasses mask his expression, but he seems downcast, almost forlorn. He takes a step toward the counter, then stops and turns back toward the shelf.

… Stacia might do another time, but not for my first time, my first night … I've got the perfect combination … the photos are going to be stunning … the ones I developed this morning are fucking awesome … especially the one where she's huddled on the floor of the van, blood running down her cheek while she begged me to let her go … oh yeah … no one but me will ever get to see them to appreciate my skill, but I'll know … the one in the car is strong and feisty. I'll pose her with the other one first so I can capture the contrast of before and after, brunette and blonde … I should have taken more shots of the first girl before she got so bloody, but hey, it was worth it … she'll be too tired to put up a fight tonight, but I'll still get some more fun out of her before I slice her throat … gotta make sure I set up the video camera just right so that it captures the look on her face as she bleeds to death …

I want to run, but my legs are numb, my body chilled. It's like my feet are chained to the floor, as if I'm stuck here, inside Matt, inside Ashley's captor — very soon to be Savannah's captor as well. Not only did he brutalize Ashley, he photographed it all. I see the photographs in his mind, and feel his pleasure at the awful, awful images.

… I loved hearing the snapping sound of the duct tape as I wrapped it around the brunette's — around Ashley's! — wrists … she struggled but I held her tight … I felt so strong, so powerful. Like a god … knowing that she's downstairs, that soon, very soon, I'll be there to take her life … it's like having a secret prize waiting for me … none of these stupid fucks has any idea that I'm a killer …

I'm Emma, I'm Matt. I'm Ashley's friend. I'm Ashley's kidnapper.

Soon to be her murderer.

I've never been inside anyone for this long.

I can't make myself move.

... Stacia looks like one of the girls at the frat party — not the girl I tried to kill, lucky twat ... there was another girl there, a little taller than Stacia, with blue eyes ... I should look her up ... I'll tell her I switched schools after the accident, that it was too hard for me 'emotionally' to stay there ... chicks suck that sort of shit up, so she'll believe it. I'll make her believe it ...

"You have a sweater, I think it's angora — it's a light green, almost a sage? Try that with this eye shadow. They'll complement each other perfectly."

Stacia blinks, her long eyelashes fluttering, and her cheeks flush. I smile inwardly, pleased at her reaction, satisfied that once again I have manipulated a woman with my charm. No, not me — that's Matt! I'm Emma!

I feel small, faint.

Nonexistent.

I — *Emma! Emma! I'm Emma!* — shiver, inside and outside, as I feel Matt in me, inside of my essence. It's like my soul has become entwined with his dirty one, as if they're wrapped around each other. I can't move, I can't get away — I'm stuck, an invisible prisoner, at the mercy of my unknowing captor. This has never happened to me before. I've touched far more people than I can remember, and I've not once had this kind of experience.

Yes I have. Over a century ago.

The last time I touched the mind of a killer.

... everything is planned ... everything is ready ... finally ... tonight is my night ...

I am Matt.

... tonight I become a murderer ...

Twelve

Matt steps away from the counter and, mercifully, out of me. I'm frozen in place even though he's moved away. My mind is filled with his mind; his thoughts, his memories — and his plans.

... the girl in the basement is going to look great next to the blonde ... before and after ... battered and whole ... I should do some shots with the warming filter I bought last week ... it would work better outside, but the weather sucks ... next time, maybe ... too bad the brunette is too worn out ... she was certainly a lot of fun ... I'll kill her first, while the other girl watches ... I'll set up the video camera for that ... this is going to be so fucking awesome ...

I take one faltering step to my right, away from Matt, who continues to chat brightly with Stacia. Everything sounds like I'm under water, hearing mumbling sounds through the liquid in my ears. I can't pull my eyes away from him, although I should move — I should run! — lest he touch me again.

More importantly, I should be helping Ashley, who must be in her body right now — flailing, desperately trying to reach the nail on the wall and rip the duct tape off her hands so she can ...

So she can beat helplessly at the zip tie binding her ankles, and wait for Matt to arrive and kill her. And then Ashley and I will watch while he kills Savannah.

... I'll have to set the lights up the way I tried them out last week ... I'll hold the knife out in front of the camera, with the girls in the background ... then zoom in on the blade ...

I shake my head, trying to get him out — out! — of my head. It's like stepping on an ant pile and having thousands of ants crawling all over you — you brush some off while others start climbing back up your legs.

Matt grins at Stacia and slaps the palm of his hand on the countertop. The sound is so loud it breaks through my haze and makes me jump. He turns and heads for the exit, his steps firm and purposeful.

I stare at his muscular shoulders as he walks away. He is so strong. Far too strong for Ashley to even dream of overpowering.

The door jingles as it shuts behind him. I stand there blinking for a minute, then dash for the basement door and fly down the stairs. I feel like I'm in a cartoon — moving in slow motion even though my feet are spinning in crazy circles.

I run and run until I finally make it to the wall, my stupid personal wall, which keeps me from reaching my friend.

She's awake, curled up on her side; the tape still binding her wrists, her ankles still tied with that plastic thing. Her face is streaked with tears and dried blood.

"Emma, Emma — are you there?" Her voice is faint. She moves her hands toward her ankles and her fingers tug feebly at the strip of plastic.

"I can' t do it, Emma, I'm sorry. I just can't. I'm so tired." Her eyes close and her voice fades so I can barely hear it.

"Tired ..."

She lies still.

Oh my Lord. Did she just die?

I press as close as I can against my invisible wall to try to see if she's still breathing, but the way she's huddled up I can't be sure one way or another. If she dies her spirit should rise up like it did before, shouldn't it? But nothing is happening. Maybe she isn't going to end up being a ghost? Maybe she'd only become a ghost if he actually killed her at the very end?

I stare at her motionless body. She doesn't deserve to die. Even if she doesn't turn into a ghost and get stuck here like me — she can't die!

She looks blurry for a moment, and then a second Ashley lifts her head up out of the first. She props herself on an elbow, then rolls away from herself and pushes herself to her feet.

"Are you dead?" My chest is as tight as if it was bound with metal like a barrel. Did I just watch her die? I should have tried harder to convince her to escape when I first found her. This is all my fault!

She peers down at her body, curled up in its pathetic little ball, then leans over and squints at her own face.

"Nope, I'm still breathing." She scoots away from herself, toward me. "But I couldn't reach that nail."

Her eyes flicker over to the wall where the inaccessible nail sticks out, defiantly offering both hope and despair.

"I tried, Emma. I tried so hard! But I just couldn't do it. I don't have the strength to stretch that far. I even tried to use my teeth to bite through the tape, but there are like a zillion layers of tape." She sniffles. "I did everything I could think of; I really did."

"Can you try again? I know it's hard, but he's coming, very soon. I — " My breath catches, and my voice drops to a whisper.

"I touched his mind."

I thought his thoughts.

I was Matt.

We stand there for a moment, the silence drowned out by the echoes of Matt's memory of Ashley sobbing, pleading, begging him to release her.

"Not very nice thoughts, were they?" she says. Her voice is light, but when I glance up and meet her gaze I can see the fear in her eyes.

"Oh Ashley. You've got to try again. I can't watch him kill you!"

Her face screws up.

"Don't you get it? I can't reach the fucking nail!" She starts to cry, tears trickling down her rosy, unblemished cheeks. I glance at her unconscious body lying on the floor, her living, bruised face still wet itself with real tears.

I desperately want her to escape, but she's right. If she can't reach the nail then we need to figure something else out. There's got to be something else to *be* figured out.

"Is that the only nail?"

She chokes down a sob.

"I — I don't know. I didn't see any others. I almost didn't see that one because it was right above my head."

"Darn it all. I can't see any more either, certainly not from where I'm stuck over here." I kick my wall. "Ow!"

She stares at me for a second, her mouth hanging open. "Oh my God, Emma."

"Oh, it's fine," I snarl. I wiggle my sore toes.

"No, no it's not. I didn't think!"

"What do you mean?"

"When I was out of my body!" She takes a step toward her body, then looks back at me. "I just wanted so badly to leave it, to get away, and forget. So I never have looked around for nails or anything except when I was inside my body! There might be a nail that I could reach if I had looked for it!"

We gape at each other, then she starts frantically searching the area near her unconscious self. She peers under the bench, then crouches down on the carpet. Her right foot sticks into her body's knees and disappears from view.

"Emma, there aren't any more nails!" she wails, her voice filled with desperation. "I don't know what to do! I don't want to die because I was stupid!"

"It doesn't have to be a nail." I try to sound calm and soothing, as if I'm not worried at all, but I can hear the waver in my voice.

"Look for something sharp — and it doesn't even have to be that sharp! All you need to do is rip the tape." She grimaces, then nods and stands up.

If we find something and she can free her hands, then what will she do? I try to block that thought.

The only thing that seems remotely promising is the end of the screw that's holding the weights on to the barbell. It's not nearly sharp enough, but it might work — maybe. One end of the barbell is on my side of the invisible wall, so I scrutinize it. It will have to do.

"Ashley, what about this?"

She scrambles over to me. "What? What about what?"

I point at the end of the screw.

"That? That's just a screw." Her voice shakes. "It's too dull — it's not going to work!"

"It *will* work. I'm sure of it." I use the tone I always used to promise Lizzie everything would be okay when she was scared. The backs of my head and my neck have that prickly feeling again.

"No, no it won't. It isn't sharp enough! I won't be able to do it! Oh my God, I'm really going to die!"

"Yes you will be able to do it. It's going to work!" I have to calm her down or there won't be enough time to find out before Matt arrives.

"Here's what I want you to do. Go back in your body and move over here, by this side of the barbell." I point to the end closest to me.

"Then lift your arms up and rip the tape on this screw. I'll be right here beside you, watching."

"But I won't be able to see you!" she cries. "When I'm in my body I can't see you! I can't do this — I need your help!"

"You won't be able to see me, but I'll be right here, right next to you. And I'll watch to make sure everything goes okay."

Although there's nothing I can do if it doesn't.

"But then what? What about my feet?" She glances at the door. "He could be here any minute!"

"We have time."

At least a little — Matt isn't stupid. He'll wait until after the store closes to bring Savannah down here.

I reach out and rest my hand on her shoulder. She doesn't feel warm, or cold — just there.

"Go on, Ashley. We're going to get you out of here."

I hope.

Ashley clasps her hands together and stares at the floor. Her fingers are clenched so tightly that her knuckles are white. She takes a deep breath.

"Okay," she mumbles. She stands there for a moment, then turns around and heads back toward her body.

Ashley kneels down next to herself and looks at her own battered face, mottled red and purple and black with bruises and blood, the one eye swollen. She reaches both hands toward her body. Right before her fingers touch her body's side she stops, her arms held out in mid-air above the living Ashley, as though she's a puppeteer, about to pull invisible strings to control her physical being.

"Emma?" she murmurs.

"I'm right here."

Her eyes don't leave her body's face.

"I'll do my best, Emma. Really. I will."

"I know."

She scrunches her eyes closed and moves her hands forward until they're invisible, hidden by her body.

Nothing happens.

After a moment her eyes open.

"It's not working anymore!" she wails. "I came down here before and did exactly the same thing, and then all of a sudden I was in — I was inside myself, and —" She swallows and stares at her knees, then whispers, "And I was awake."

She stays like that for a moment, then turns toward me, her brow furrowed. As if *I'm* going to know what to do!

"What's wrong, Emma? Why isn't it working?"

I bite my lip and try to think. Now that we've finally come up with something to try, can we really not get her back in her own body?

"You've done this several times now, right? Is there anything you can think of that you're doing differently now?" I try to sound matter-of-fact, as if there's some simple formula that she's merely forgotten. I feel myself trembling, and hope she doesn't notice.

What could possibly be different?

She frowns and balls her hands into fists, then taps them lightly on her thighs. Tap tap tap. Tap tap tap.

I rest my right hand on the invisible stone wall in between us.

"I only did it on purpose the one time, earlier tonight." She nods her head.

"I came downstairs and looked at myself. It — I — it seemed like I was asleep, so I put my hand on, uh, um, on my shoulder, and then I was back inside myself." The tapping has become more of a smacking. "And it just worked. But this time it's not."

"What about the times before that?" Could the one time she went back on purpose have coincided with when her body became conscious?

Her eyes flit from side to side.

"I don't know. It's all fuzzy. I just tried to go back the one time — the others just kind of happened."

Why would a spirit return to its body without planning to? If she was unconscious, and then her body woke up all on its own — well, then her spirit would have to return. I think.

"I —" she starts, then snaps her mouth shut and stares at her knees.

I wait for a minute, but she doesn't say anything else. Did she remember something? What is she not telling me?

"Ashley, what is it?"

She looks at me askance. "Some of the other times I came back *he* was here."

"What do you mean?" How could Matt being here be related to her reentering her body?

She takes a deep breath before responding. "I think that he hurt me. I mean the non-ghost me. And so I had to come back those times because he hurt me so badly it woke me up." Her eyes flick toward her body, then settle back on me.

I keep my face impassive, but I seethe inside as I picture Matt kicking her while she laid unconscious on the floor, forcing her spirit to return to her body, to wake up, just so he could abuse her again. I can't believe I ever had a crush on such an abhorrent human being.

… works every time …

Jamie Ferguson

Even if it would wake her up, neither Ashley nor I can cause her body any pain, much less enough to rouse it. But she went back once on purpose — unless that was a coincidence. I clench my jaw. She did; she said so. Which means she can do it again!

I narrow my eyes, determinedly ignoring the possibility that it was mere circumstance.

"Ashley, when you came down here earlier, did you think of anything in particular?"

"No!" She smacks the floor with her hands. "This is it! This is exactly what I did before!"

"Calm down!" I snap. Her eyes grab mine. "Take a deep breath." She sucks in a huge gulp of air and holds it.

What happened to the nonchalant girl I met a few days ago, the one who said she'd just as soon become a ghost? The imminence of her death has transformed the Ashley I know.

It's only been a few days, but it feels as if I've known her forever.

"Remember how it felt to be inside your body. Remember being tied up, remember the pain —" Her mouth drops open, and I hurry to explain myself. "It's part of how your body feels right now, part of your reality — remembering it might help you connect with the part of you that's in the physical world."

I cringe inside as I think of what I'm asking Ashley to do.

"Focus on yourself, on *all* of you. Think about what has happened to you, on how your body feels. You need to convince your body to rouse itself out of unconsciousness."

I tighten my hands into fists, digging my fingernails into the palms of my hands. Please, oh please, let this work! If it doesn't …

My nails are pressing against my skin so hard I'd be bleeding if I weren't a ghost.

"Okay," Ashley mutters. She looks at her body, supine on the floor, then closes her eyes.

I cross my arms, my fists still clenched tight. Matt will be here soon — very soon. This is our last chance. Ashley's last chance, and probably Savannah's. If Ashley can escape she'll save herself, and her friend, too. Or they might both die.

My stomach feels as if it's tied in a million tight little knots.

Ashley kneels down again, her eyes still closed, and stretches her arms out toward her body. Her hands are shaking. She pauses for a moment, then takes a breath and moves forward, into herself. First her hands disappear inside her body, then her forearms, and then —

She's gone. Only one Ashley remains, lying on her side on the floor.

I press my hands flat against my wall and watch, wishing I wasn't so damn *helpless*.

Ashley's body — Ashley, now — sighs. A deep, weary sigh.

"I'm here, Emma," she says. Her voice is low and scratchy.

It worked. She's back in her body — it really worked.

She rolls from her right side onto her stomach, her bound arms underneath her, then slowly starts to pull herself up to lean against the barbell that her legs are wrapped around. She uses the metal pole for leverage, but it's clearly a lot of work, especially since her ankles are tied and she can't use her feet.

My knees were scraped and bruised, like the rest of my body. I dragged myself across the hard dirt floor, using my elbows to pull myself along. With every movement I could feel pain where the floor was pressing against my bruises. Because my ankles were tied together I had to move both legs at once. It was difficult to keep my balance. My broken wrist hurt so badly that I almost collapsed because it was hard to keep my weight on that elbow.

The scent of damp earth is strong in my nostrils.

She drags herself, inch by brutal inch, until she's propped up against the big, round weights on the end of the barbell. She's completely on my side of the old wall now. She grunts and collapses, panting hard. Her bruises seem much worse this close up. I think her eye is a little less swollen than when I first found her, but it's hard to be sure. Even if it is, it still looks awful.

I kneel down next to her. I hope she has the strength to rip the tape. After that ... Her ankles would still be tied together, but she could crawl over to the door. Did he lock it? He must have. And the door at the top of the stairs is locked too. I pinch my lips together, overwhelmed by all the obstacles that must be surmounted before Ashley will be free.

One thing at a time, Mama used to say.

Ashley grunts and pushes herself to a sitting position, then lifts her arms up and begins scraping the duct tape wrapped around her wrists against the end of the screw that's attaching the weights to the barbell. Her movements are slow and jerky. I can tell she's tired, but the tape is tearing. Well, not tearing, exactly — it's more like the tape is being sawed off. Slowly. It's going to take a while, but she's doing it.

"Come on, Ashley!" She can't hear me, but I cheer her on anyway.

Ashley pulls her arms back and forth, her battered, swollen face filled with weary determination. She seems to be getting weaker. She wasn't moving quickly to begin with, and it's almost as though she's slowing while I watch. I look from the reluctantly ripping tape to her face, then back again.

Little prickles run across my shoulders as I think of what Matt has planned for Ashley.

Every once in a while she hits the screw with her hand and scrapes her skin. When she does she makes a little whimpering sound that tears at my heart. If only I could do something. She's almost there. I grit my teeth and try to will her energy. Just a little further ...

"Emma?" she murmurs, her voice so faint I can barely hear her. "Emma, I — I —"

She collapses on the floor. Her eyes are closed, but I can hear her ragged breathing. What happened? I lean over to peer at her face, then leap back as the spirit Ashley sits up.

"Hey, give me some room!" she snaps.

Oh no — she's unconscious again. She can't escape unless she's in her body.

The spirit Ashley scoots away from herself and regards me gloomily.

"Ashley, you did great! But you have to go back! I'm sure you're exhausted. But it's ripping!"

She sighs, and pokes tentatively at her body with a finger. Her finger slides into her body and out of our sight.

"Yeah. It sure is."

Now that she's figured out how to get back in her body we just need to focus. We're going to get her out of here.

"You're so close —" My voice trails off as I notice her expression.

"I can't do it, Emma." She rubs her eyes. "Just getting the tape to start to tear took all the strength I had." She glances at her body, then at the floor.

"Of course you can do it!"

Ashley shakes her head. Her face is sad, so terribly sad.

"Sure you do! It's hard, but you'll be able to do it. I know you can!"

"Emma, my body passed out!" Her voice becomes strident, and her eyes are wet. "Ripping that off on that stupid screw would take another hour even if I hadn't been lying down here for days! *I just can't do it!*" She buries her face in her hands.

I stare at the barbell, my mind numb. She's right — there's no way. There's truly no way.

I kneel on the floor next to Ashley's body. Poor thing. All this pain, all this horror, and now she's going to have to watch herself be killed. If he manages to get her conscious — and from what I know of Matt now, he will certainly try — then she won't just be watching. She'll be living it. Feeling it. Just like I did.

I can't let that happen to Ashley.

I reach my hand out and touch her body. And then I open my eyes.

Ashley's eyes.

Thirteen

The left eye is so swollen that it only opens up a crack. There's a sharp pain deep in my right side, and every breath sends shooting pains throughout my body. My head feels like a wagon wheel ran over it, it's hard to see with the one eye mostly closed, especially in the dim light, and sounds I hear are muffled as if I'm hearing everything through a feather pillow. But at the same time —

— I feel *alive!*

Every sensation is magnified; every pain, every touch, every smell, every sound. The worn carpet is rough against the skin of my arm, and there's a tight ache across my shoulders from sawing off the tape. The scent from the open bag of chips on the mattress is as strong as it would be if my nose were jammed in the bag. My stomach grumbles with hunger, like a little lion roaring in my belly.

I'm alive! I'm in Ashley's body! *I am Ashley.*

But I'm not really Ashley — she isn't here. This isn't like all the other times when I've touched the living. Something is missing. *She's* missing. Her body is an empty shell, vacant without her mind. I can't read her thoughts, I can't feel her essence. The spirit Ashley is watching me right now, but I can't see her anymore.

Her body feels much like mine, yet it's different. It's like borrowing a coat that is almost, but not exactly, the right size; where you're comfortable enough to forget it belongs to someone else, but in the back of your mind you're always aware that it doesn't quite fit.

A car passes by on the street outside, the headlights briefly brightening the room through the little windows on the street side of the basement. It isn't Matt, but he's coming. Soon.

I raise my head to look at my borrowed shape through my good eye. My legs are encased in bloodstained denim, the blue fabric splotched with dark red. I wriggle my toes and twist my feet. My left foot is cold without its shoe.

I start to sit up, but a sharp pain stabs through my right side, and I collapse on the carpet. Oh, it hurts, it hurts so much!

But at the same time the pain is welcome, almost pleasurable. It is something I can truly feel. It's something *real.*

I use my arms to maneuver myself onto my left side, then squirm around until I can lever myself up. My breaths are short and shallow, and I have to move slowly, but I finally coerce myself into a sitting position. I grab on to the weights attached to the barbell and drag myself over until I'm positioned right where the nut is holding the screw in place. They're both sticky with tape residue.

I try to get my wrists positioned so I can finish ripping the tape, and my fingers brush the striated metal of the screw. It seems as if I can feel every groove in the screw — if I tried I think I could count them. My breathing improves, each breath becoming deeper, more secure, than the last. Maybe I — I mean, maybe Ashley doesn't have a broken rib after all? I feel strong, so amazingly strong. How can this be? I'm in Ashley's body — she's worn, tired, just like she'd said. I can feel her body's exhaustion, the fatigue so enervating I now understand why she couldn't do anything more after sawing through the duct tape.

But her exhaustion doesn't have the same effect on me.

I'm alive!

The energy of life — *life!* — is giving me strength. Blood courses through Ashley's veins — real blood, in a real body. Her heart beats in my chest. With each breath I follow the air as it goes down my throat, into my lungs. It's still difficult to breathe deeply, but it's easier than it was a minute ago. The pain of my injuries is intense, but the life force fills me with vigor. I lap it up like a horse at a drinking trough after a long, hard ride.

I drag the tape across the screw, back and forth. In spite of my surprising energy, it's a slow process, but I keep at it. As strong as I am I'm sure I could move these weights if I had to. I'll get the tape off, and then Ashley will be free.

And then —

I'll leave her body. She'll be alive; I'll return to being a ghost, trapped here forever. Intangible. Ineffectual. Alone.

You could stay …

The thought pops into my head, unbidden. Could I stay? What would happen to Ashley if I didn't leave her body? My throat feels tight.

I'd be alive!

No! I can't steal her body. How could I even think about such a thing? Besides, not only would it be wrong, I don't even know if it would work.

But what if it did? Ashley would become a ghost, but I — I wouldn't be a ghost anymore.

No. I grit my teeth and try to shoulder away my jealousy, my envy of Ashley's life.

A metallic sound from the direction of the parking lot jars me out of my argument with myself. Is Matt here? I have to work faster. I twist and tug on the duct tape, my living energy boundless. I have to get it off.

The tape is impervious to my plight.

I scrape and pull and suddenly the last section of tape gives way. I'm pushing so hard that my hands fly forward and smack into the heavy weight on the end of the barbell. The ends of the tape flop to the side, like a flower opening from a bud. The ripped tape is still stuck to my wrists; I pull my hands apart and watch the tape fall to the floor.

There's a clunk outside.

Panicked, I sit up straighter, then fall back as pain spikes through my right side again. I try to keep myself from toppling over, but having my ankles — Ashley's ankles, I remind myself firmly — tied up like this makes it difficult. I grab on to one of the weights to try to keep my balance, and my eyes fasten on the shoebox that's next to the stack of magazines. It looks like the one Jimmy Peterson kept his treasures in, although surely it can't be the same one after all this time.

I use the pole of the barbell to pull myself closer. The metal is cold and hard. I peer at the shoebox through Ashley's one good eye. It was so much easier to see when I had the benefit of ghost sight.

Something slams hard against the outside of the door. A low, male voice mutters something — I can't make out his words, but the tone is cold and commanding. Matt is finally here.

I lean forward and grasp the cardboard box with my left hand. I rip the lid off with shaking hands. The box is packed full of a mishmash of things.

The door handle rattles.

I heard a thump from above, then a light shone through the crack underneath the door, brightening the darkness of my prison. I froze, squinting, my elbows resting on the step above my head, my hands pressed against the cool stone. I was halfway up — halfway to freedom. But I had to get back down. If he caught me trying to escape —

My heart is beating like mad. I have to stay calm, I can't let myself panic — I have to stay calm for Ashley. And Savannah. And all of the other girls that would surely follow. Calm. I rummage in the box. Lots of marbles. A geode. A desiccated stick of gum.

There are scuffling sounds outside of the door, and something bangs against it again. Savannah must not be cooperating. A ball of twine. An old bullet.

An old flint arrowhead.

I grab it and wince as it digs into my skin. Maybe it will be sharp enough. I twist around so I can reach my ankles and start scraping the sharpest end against the plastic binding with all my might.

There is a heavy, very solid thump against the door, as if something — or someone — was thrown against it. I hear the key in the door.

The handle turns.

The flint point slices through the plastic at the same time the door opens.

He caught me trying to escape just once. I was halfway up the stairs when he flung the door open, the light from his lantern so bright I felt half-blind. He must have been waiting for me with the lantern covered, listening at the door while I struggled up the stairs. He stomped down to me, then pushed me so I fell, tumbling over and over on the stone steps all the way to the bottom, unable to catch myself with my arms and legs tied as they were. He followed me down and dragged me into the center of the room, flinging me on the pile of straw, then he hit me until I couldn't think straight. He didn't kill me for another three days.

Matt thrusts Savannah through the door and into the room ahead of me. Savannah lands on her right side with a solid thump. Her arms are bound behind her back, and there's a piece of duct tape over her mouth. Her pretty blonde hair is mussed, and there's a splotch of blood on her lavender sweater, probably from the scrape on her left temple. Her ankles are taped together, the duct tape wrapped around the legs of her jeans.

Matt rips the tape from her mouth, then pulls her up and shoves her toward the bed. She lands on the mattress, bouncing slightly from the impact. He flips the light switch next to the door and the two floor lamps turn on, their harsh light brightening the room, reflecting off the dark wood paneling on the walls and the worn silver metal of the barbell. My eyes struggle to adjust.

Matt slams the door shut, then sees me. He grins. I stare back at him, at his mop of golden curls, his broad shoulders, and his face — so achingly familiar, yet now so foreign. His hair is slightly tousled, but he's dazzlingly handsome as always. My killer looked like a bad guy from the start, but Matt doesn't look like a murderer at all. I was so sure Ashley had been abducted by Edward, so sure. I was so wrong.

He locks the door, the key clicking softly as it turns, then he puts the key in the left front pocket of his jeans.

"Get up," he orders. He sounds colder than a lake in the mountains, and there isn't an ounce of emotion in his voice. His icy blue eyes watch me. Savannah squirms on the mattress. My shoulders, sore from the effort of removing the tape from Ashley's wrists, ache in sympathy.

Matt's eyes narrow. "You heard me. Now."

"Get up," he ordered. I pushed myself up until I was on my hands and knees. I fell over on my side, then tried again, somehow keeping my balance long enough to rise to my feet. He coughed and spit on the floor, his spittle landing with a loud splat. I stood there, swaying slightly — my ankles had been tied for days, and my legs were wobbly.

"Get over here now, because you won't like it if I have to come get you."

I swallowed. I didn't want to walk toward him, but knew

what would happen if I didn't. I managed to take two steps in his direction before my knees buckled and I collapsed. He cackled as he strode over to me.

I struggle to my feet, my legs shaky and weak, the pain in my side dull but persistent. I stand up, lightheaded, and try to keep my balance. Where is all the energy I had just a few minutes ago? Is this how Ashley felt after she tried to saw off the tape? I realize Ashley is taller than I was — I've spent so much time following Matt around like a little puppy that I can tell her eyes see him from a slightly different angle than my own.

Out of the corner of my uninjured eye I can see Savannah staring at me. I'd forgotten that she didn't know Ashley was down here — and that Ashley didn't know that Matt was going to kidnap Savannah.

Savannah struggles to a sitting position, the bedframe creaking as she moves. Matt glances at her, then backhands her across the face. She falls back down on the mattress.

He motions to me with his left hand, his movements short and tight. He appears very controlled, very cool. This isn't the charming, kind, funny Matt I've come to know — or thought I knew. I feel dizzy, my thoughts all in a jumble. I don't know what else to do, so I take one unsteady step forward, then another. Icy fingers wrap around my heart as I realize I don't know how to leave Ashley's body. What will happen if Matt kills Ashley's body with me in it? Will I die — again?

I hit my invisible wall in mid-step. I'd completely forgotten about it, but it's as sturdy and inflexible as ever. As my foot — Ashley's foot — goes through the wall I ooze out of Ashley's body. It's like holding a shawl wrapped tight around yourself, then dropping it and feeling the fabric glide on your skin as it falls away.

As I move back into my ghostly form all my senses are dampened. The light seems dimmer, the air less dusty and dry. The pain in my side vanishes, the dull ache of my many bruises gone. I'm me again, no longer a visitor in someone else's body. No longer alive.

Ashley's body collapses on the floor directly in front of Matt. He doesn't move a muscle as she falls. There's no emotion on his face, not even when her head hits the base of one of the floor lamps with a loud thunk. Great. Ashley doesn't need Matt to kill her — by forgetting about the stupid wall and letting her fall and smack her head like that I've probably done the job for him.

"Hey!" Ashley's spirit is kneeling next to her body on the other side of the wall, her brow furrowed. "Why did you leave my body? You let me hit my head!"

We both stare corporeal at the physical, tangible Ashley, crumpled up in a sad little pile next to the lamp.

Ashley stands up and moves toward me to get out of Matt's way as he walks toward her body.

I sigh, my earlier hopes crushed. "The original house ended here." I move my hand back and forth next to where my wall sits, impenetrable and invisible. "I can't leave it — apparently not even in your body."

I'm empty and numb. Being alive again, even in such grim circumstances, was like being shot full with lightning. Now I'm like an old, pressed flower — my petals are dry and brittle, their once bright, vibrant color faded away to the hue of pale parchment.

"Oh, Emma," Ashley says softly. "I'm going to die. And Savannah too. I can't believe he caught her too."

We watch as Matt grabs Ashley's limp, lifeless arms and drags her across the carpet, depositing her on the floor next to the bed. Savannah's eyes dash madly around the room, looking for a way out, for someone to save her. I peek at Ashley. Her face looks like mine must. Helpless. Hopeless. Scared.

His booted feet thumped as he came down the stairs, his steps slow and solid on the stone. He was grinning. In another time, another place, the gaps in his teeth would have looked almost comical, but here they merely added to his menacing appearance. "I bet you like surprises, little missy. And have I got one for you." He had something clasped in his hand, his fingers clenched tight around it.

Matt reaches underneath the couch and pulls out a zip tie, then walks slowly over to Savannah. His expression hasn't altered the entire time. It's like his features were carved by a glacier, ground into place and now fixed, unchanging. Savannah scrabbles away from him as he approaches the bed, but she is only able to move so far before her back is against the wall.

Matt reaches out for her feet. She tries to kick at him, making frantic noises that are muffled by her gag, but her motions are awkward with her legs taped together, and he's fast and strong on top of that. He uses his knee to pin her down while he wraps the plastic strip around her ankles. With her arms tied behind her back she can't do anything else but writhe helplessly.

He pulls the tie tight, then steps back and smiles. It's the first emotion he's showed the entire time, and the look of pleasure and satisfaction on his face is nothing at all like the Matt I thought I knew. There is no charm in his smile now. He rips the duct tape off her legs and tosses it aside. He inspects Savannah for a moment, then grins.

"Definitely better than tape." He pats Savannah's booted foot, then unlocks the door and heads out to his car, leaving the door partway open. The air coming in from outside is cool and crisp and smells faintly of pine.

"Get back in your body!" I yell at Ashley. "You can escape while the door is open!"

Savannah wiggles around until she gets her legs off the bed. She tries to stand up, but loses her balance and manages to fling herself to the floor instead. She makes a loud thud as she lands on her side right next to Ashley's body.

"How can I escape?" Ashley snaps. "He's five feet from the door! Have you noticed the shape I'm in? You were in my body — there's no way I'll be able to get past him!" She wrings her hands together.

I look from the pathetic little lump of her body, sprawled on the floor next to Savannah, to the vibrant, angry, intangible Ashley who is standing next to me. The prickling feeling is stronger. My neck feels like a pincushion stuck full of a thousand needles.

"You —" I falter. "I don't know if you can. But maybe you can distract him and Savannah will be able to."

Ashley stares at me, then nods her head. She starts to move toward her body, then freezes as Matt comes back through the door. He's carrying two large, black bags and a contraption that consists of a piece of black metal attached to three black and silver poles. He shuts the door with his knee, then locks it and turns and walks past the bed, ignoring the squirming Savannah, his arms full of his collection of things. The key slips out of his hand and falls to the floor as he walks past Ashley's body; he doesn't appear to notice. The bright silver metal glints in the light as the key drops. It lands on the carpet, and bounces under the bedframe and out of sight.

"Fuck. I was too slow." Ashley pulls at the hem of her blouse.

Matt deposits his peculiar assortment next to the wall across from the couch. He picks up the old television set and moves it to the southeast corner of the room, then does the same with the books stacked next to where the television was sitting. After clearing the area he grabs the metal frame and one of the plastic tubes from next to the sofa and carries them over to the now empty north wall. He props up the frame, then opens the tube and pulls out a long roll of pale blue vinyl.

"What the hell he doing?" Ashley asks. She moves past me and sits down on the couch, pulling her feet up on the worn cushion and wrapping her arms around her knees. Matt attaches the vinyl to the top of frame, and unrolls it until the end of the fabric rests on the floor.

"He's going to take photographs," I mutter.

"What? Photos of what?"

"You and Savannah. He's crazy, in case you haven't noticed. Most sane people don't kidnap and murder other people."

"I know that!" She snaps. "But what is the point of taking pictures?"

I shake my head, trying not to think about what I saw in Matt's mind earlier. He rummages in one of the bags, then walks by the spirit Ashley carrying a large camera in one hand and the black and silver gizmo in the other. She scowls at him.

"Well, I'm sure it makes sense in his disgusting little world."

I watch, numb and impotent, as he sets up the metallic device. It turns out the poles are the legs of a tripod. He places the camera on top of the tripod and fiddles with it for a few minutes. Ashley glowers at him from the couch, her arms still hugging her legs. Her lower lip is trembling.

The room is quiet except for the occasional click from whatever it is that Matt is doing with the camera and soft thumps as Savannah continues to try to escape. She's managed to crawl over to the door and is standing up, her back to the door so she can reach the doorknob with her bound hands. She's looking around the room while she tugs at the locked handle. Tears stream down her face; her expression is beaten and forlorn. Matt ignores her. I watch Savannah pull feebly at the handle for a moment, then I whirl toward Ashley.

"Ashley!" I whisper. She glances at me, then turns back to watch Matt. "What about the key?"

"What about it?" Her voice breaks.

"It bounced underneath the bed when it fell. If you get back in your body you can grab it while he's over here."

Ashley's mouth falls open. She leaps up.

"Do you really think I can? But —" Her head swings from side to side. "But he's *right there*. There's no way I can grab the key, make it to the door, unlock it, and escape." She pauses and looks at Savannah. "Besides," she snarls. "You managed to let me fall and hit my head. I probably have a concussion now. That's not going to help."

She brushes her hair behind an ear, her hands shaking so badly that her movements are all jerky.

"Oh, fuck it," she mutters and rushes over to her body. She glances over her shoulder at Matt, who's rummaging in one of his collection of bags. "Will I have enough time? Oh, Goddammit — why didn't I think of this before! Maybe I can at least buy some time for Savannah!"

Ashley kneels in front of herself and reaches out just like she did before, her face screwed up. I perch on the arm of the couch and cross the fingers on both my hands. Ashley's body is exhausted — will she be able to reach the key, get to the door, and unlock it? All while Matt's back is turned? My chest tightens.

"Come on, come on," Ashley mutters. Nothing seems to be happening. She opens her eyes. "I can't do it! Why can't I do it?"

"Maybe you're trying too hard? Isn't that what it seemed to be the last time?" I glance at the lamp, feeling guilty even though I didn't mean to let her fall like that. What if she's so deeply unconscious that she's in a coma, and she *can't* wake herself up?

Matt walks past me and over to Savannah, who is still tugging futilely on the door handle.

"It's too late anyhow," Ashley says bitterly.

We watch as Matt wraps his big hands around Savannah's ankles, pulling her to the floor. He drags her over to the north wall. Her blonde hair trails behind her, and I can see her fingers twisting as she passes me. She doesn't seem to have made any progress in getting the tape off her wrists.

Matt props Savannah up in a sitting position, her back leaning up against the blue backdrop, her hair a static-filled golden cloud around her head. He turns back toward Ashley's body and Savannah flops over on one side. Matt grabs her shoulders, repositions her against the wall, then smacks her face so hard it sounds like a whip cracking. He moves back to Ashley's lifeless body, throws her over his shoulder, and carries her across the room. He places her on Savannah's right, leaning Ashley's head against Savannah's shoulder so that she doesn't fall over. Savannah's eyes are huge as she looks at her unconscious friend. A large, angry red mark has appeared on the right side of her face where Matt hit her; it's a big, rosy handprint.

Matt moves back to the camera and observes the two girls. "Very nice," he murmurs. He runs his fingers through his curly hair, then pulls some lights out of one of the black bags and begins setting them up so that they brighten the area where he's posed his victims.

The bruises on Ashley's face are a dark reddish-purple, making her uninjured skin look deathly white in comparison. For a moment I see Lizzie's face superimposed on Ashley's. It's just like when I can feel the stone walls of the old house through the present-day drywall.

Fourteen

I shake free from the odd image my mind has created and focus on Ashley standing next to me. Tears are streaming down her cheeks.

My eyes flick back to Matt's composition just as the camera's flash goes off, momentarily filling the room with a dazzling brightness. After the light fades away, everything seems dim and murky. Lizzie's face is gone; the unconscious Ashley looks like herself again, pathetic and helpless, her head propped up on Savannah's right shoulder, her long brown hair hanging forward, hiding part of her bruised and beaten face.

I rub the back of my neck, where the prickling has become a kind of tingling. Savannah shifts her weight to one side and Ashley's lifeless body follows, slumping more heavily on Savannah. The top button on Ashley's blouse must have come off when Matt moved her. The bright, happy fabric hangs loose, revealing the curve of her left breast.

Not only are we going to have to watch Ashley and Savannah be murdered, we're going to have to watch as Matt photographs the whole thing. I'm surprised he doesn't have a video camera, then remember that he does. It must be squirreled away in one of his bags, waiting to be pulled it out to record his dastardly deeds. Why doesn't he just kill these poor girls now? Why does he have to prolong the fear, the frustration — the horror? How dare he. How dare he toy with these girls?

I realize suddenly that he's moved Ashley's body so she's back within my walls. If Ashley can't re-enter her body, maybe I can, now that I can reach her. I can't get to the key — it's well past my wall — but I can try to distract him so Savannah can get it and hopefully unlock the door, if I can find a way to give her enough time.

I storm over to Ashley's body and touch her arm. Then I open my — Ashley's eyes.

The left eye seems a little less swollen than before. I can actually see through it now, although not very well. I pull myself off of Savannah's shoulder. My head feels strangely heavy, and there's an ache on my right temple that must be from landing on the base of the floor lamp. I sense Savannah's eyes on me, and I hear the soft sound of her breathing. The pain in my side doesn't seem as sharp as it was earlier, or else it simply doesn't hurt as much in this position.

Matt is crouching on the floor by the tripod, fiddling with his camera. He glances over at me, and our eyes meet, so he knows I'm conscious. He must not think much of me because he turns his attention back to his camera, dismissing me as a threat to his plans. But I know something that Matt doesn't know, something he could never expect. Ashley may be weak, beaten and battered, worn out from days without food or water, but *I'm* in her body — and in her body I'm strong. I'm *alive*.

I stretch my shoulders and back, exploring the state of Ashley's body. Can I run? If I head up the stairs Matt will chase me, leaving Savannah alone, maybe even for a few minutes. The door at the top of the steps is locked — that's as far as I'll be able to get, assuming Matt doesn't catch me sooner. Will that give Savannah enough time? And if by some miracle she does escape, what will happen to Ashley?

There's nothing else I can do, so it will have to be enough. If I don't do anything at all, both girls will be dead soon. At the very least I'll be able to save Savannah. I wanted a friend. I wanted Ashley to stay here with me. I've never before felt so awful knowing that I was going to get something I'd hoped for.

"Savannah!" I hiss her name, trying hard to keep my voice soft and low so Matt can't hear what I'm saying, although I'm sure he knows I'm talking to her. It's difficult to whisper with my lips as swollen as they are. They feel big and fat, and they're terribly tender. I run my tongue across them, wincing as it reaches an especially sore spot.

Savannah's eyes meet mine. Her arms and shoulders continue to make slight, jerky movements as she attempts to free her wrists.

"The key is on the floor under the bed, right by where Ash — where I was lying before." Her eyes flit to the far side of the room, then back to me. I glance down at the zip tie holding her ankles, constricting her movement. She's not going to get there very fast. "I'll distract him."

But how? He's too close. I need him to move a little further away so that I'll have a better chance at getting all the way to the top of the stairs. How am I going to convince him to move away from me and my path out of the room?

I set my shoulders. I'm the only one here who isn't in any danger. I have to do whatever I can that might let Savannah escape, no matter what happens to me. Because he can't kill *me*.

I take a deep breath and close my eyes. I was Matt for a brief moment earlier in the day. *I thought his thoughts.* I cringe inside as I remember what it was like to be him, but maybe I can buy some time by telling him things he won't expect Ashley to know, things only he knows. If I can keep his attention for even just a little while I might be able to find a way to get him to go back toward the door to give me more of a head start.

"Matt," I call. My voice is scratchy and weak. Matt glances up from his camera, his eyebrows raised. I wonder if he ever told Ashley his name.

"Why do you want to kill us?"

I think back to being in Matt, back to being Matt. I was inside his mind, but I don't know why he wants to be a murderer. This is what he's wanted to do for a long time, so long that maybe even he doesn't know his own motivations. He thinks of this as the next stage — he's killed plenty of animals already.

I take a deep breath and try to block out those memories, then remember that I *have* to open up to everything I can recall in case it helps. I'll have plenty of time later to think about how repugnant he is.

He chuckles. His laughter is deep and throaty, a lovely, warm sound, the kind of laughter that makes you want to join in. How can he be so charming, yet at the same time so hideously evil?

"Why not?"

He reaches over to adjust one of the lights, squinting at us as he shines the bright light first one way, and then another. The outline of his biceps is visible through his shirt as his arm moves back and forth.

He was thinking about his father earlier — a hard-working, hard-drinking lawyer who was never satisfied with anything Matt did. Matt excelled in sports, but was never good enough for his father. He did well in school, but that wasn't good enough either.

"It's because of your father, isn't it?" I don't know if his father has anything to do with Matt's insane desire to become a murderer. Lots of people have bad relationships with their fathers, but if they all ended up killers the population would be significantly lower. Besides, didn't I hear in a movie that most serial killers have bad relationships with their mothers?

A drop of sweat trickles down the side of my face. I haven't sweated since I was alive. It leaves a tickly feeling in its wake. Matt is staring at me. I have to come up with something to keep his attention. What?

I swallow. The sensation is thick, palpable. Real. All the things I feel as a ghost are trivial compared to how it feels to be alive. Having a real body is distracting. I need to pay attention. I need to buy more time for Savannah. I have to — I have to think like Matt. I have to focus on the memory of *being* Matt, on what I read of his essence.

Why was he thinking about his father before? My foot is falling asleep, so I move it and then wince as a ray of pain shoots up my side.

Matt was thinking about a party. But it's so fuzzy — oh, what if I can't remember anything? I have to; I have to keep him distracted. He was … He was thinking about a girl.

A pretty girl. Long, strawberry blonde hair. Young. Probably my age, nineteen or twenty. She had a short skirt, really short. And high-heeled sandals.

"What the fuck are you talking about?" I've never before seen Matt sneer. The expression completely alters his features, and for the first time he looks like the villain I now know he is.

"Well," I blurt, trying to focus on the faint, secondhand memories. He was — it was …

Matt. Matt. I was Matt.

It was a fraternity party. His fraternity. She was a girl he'd seen around campus, and when she walked — or, more accurately, stumbled — in to the room where he was drinking with his friends, he decided to take advantage of the situation. But he hadn't planned it out — it was a rash decision. He was lucky that everyone else was so drunk they couldn't remember things clearly the next day. He's been extra careful this time, planning his abduction of first Ashley, then Savannah, down to every excruciating detail. Every detail but one.

Me.

"You're angry with your father because he won't pay for you to go back to school after what happened at the fraternity party." I hold his gaze. "You know he knows what you tried to do."

Matt freezes, his hand on the lamp. I've got his attention. That's great, but how am I going to convince him to move away long enough for me to run?

I glance over at the west side of the room. Is there something there I can convince him he needs? Both black bags are next to him — maybe there's something he needs to complete his horrible posing? I drag my gaze back to his.

"Nothing happened at the fraternity," he snarls. "I left earlier that night, I told him that. Same as I told the cops." He sets his jaw. "How —" he starts, then closes his mouth and stares at me. His beautiful gray-blue eyes are as cold as the sky in winter.

I'm Matt, I tell myself hurriedly. What would Matt think? What is he thinking right now? I have to be careful. If I make him angry he might kill me — Ashley — before I have a chance to run.

"How do I know about that night?" I smile even though it makes my swollen lips hurt. No one knows what really happened except for Matt — and now me, with my stolen memories. The attempted murder was interrupted at the last possible second and the girl was found, unconscious, by some of her friends. She was bruised and beaten, with three broken ribs, no panties, and a rope tied around her neck.

Matt escaped by climbing out a window and jumping into a tree. His fraternity was shut down, but he wasn't caught. He'd worn gloves so there were no fingerprints on anything that could be tied to him — and while his fingerprints were found at the scene he was able to explain them away very easily because the party had been at his fraternity house.

Matt finished out the semester, but without his father's money he couldn't afford to pay his tuition for the next year. And then ... He ended up here, working at the store. Followed around every day by a lovesick ghost.

"How do I know you attacked that girl, then tried to kill her?"

Matt's expression doesn't change, but I feel Savannah's body tense up next to mine. Matt had enjoyed hurting Ashley much more than the girl at the party. Ashley was sober when he kidnapped her, aware of what was happening, awake when he hurt her. The other girl had been roaring drunk, and had passed out after the first blow.

"Because —" Might as well tell him the truth. "Because I'm a ghost."

His eyes narrow.

"Those bruises look pretty real to me."

He adjusts the lamp slightly, but keeps an eye on me. I can tell he doesn't believe me, but he doesn't need to. Dammit, how can I distract him long enough for Savannah to reach the door?

"This isn't my body." He raises an eyebrow. "I was, um —" I pause. I glance down at myself — at Ashley — then look up at him.

"I've been dead for over a hundred years."

I almost said I was killed, but I stopped myself before the words came out.

"Really." His voice is flat. He definitely doesn't believe me. But who would? "Prove it."

Prove it. Prove that I'm a ghost. I take a deep breath, feeling the air enter my nose and flow all the way down to fill my lungs.

I can't even remember what breathing felt like as a ghost.

It wasn't really breathing anyway.

Maybe I could make something up, like tell him I'm buried under the floor by the door, or even tell him that there's gold there instead. Or maybe in the wall, since the floor is made of concrete. That might work. Although Matt probably would be more interested in bones than gold. I only need it to work for a minute, just long enough for me to start running.

"Underneath that wall —" I point directly behind him, then pause. This is stupid. What am I expecting? He's not going to want to dig up my bones.

"Underneath all these walls, there's stone. This room used to have stone walls, and the floor was earth."

Cold, damp earth.

Without thinking I start to bite my lip, then wince as my teeth graze my sore lips. I should just run up the stairs right now. If I'm fast enough I'll be able to get to the top. He'll come after me and carry me back down — but I can fight him. I can make it take longer so that Savannah has a decent chance.

I think.

He chuckles. "All the houses around here were built with stone-walled basements." He leans forward and his voice deepens. "So my little ghost … how did you die?" The intensity of his stare makes me shiver.

I swallow. "Uh. The plague."

Is that even plausible? Did people get the plague in

Colorado in my day? My legs are stretched out in front of me. I pull them back toward my torso, hugging my knees to my chest, trying to act nonchalant while I ready myself to run.

"Uh-huh." He smirks. "I don't believe you."

"Well ..." Did he think about anything else earlier that could help? I can't remember his thoughts clearly. I was so numb when I was inside his mind that everything is running all together.

"That party —"

He waves his hand dismissively.

"You knowing about that proves nothing. And if you *do* know anything then I have even more reason to kill you."

He smiles, his perfect teeth shiny and white in the bright light.

"Even if you *are* a ghost you're still in that body. I saw you wince earlier. You can feel pain. And you can be murdered." His eyes narrow and he looks at me with something akin to hunger. "You were murdered the first time you died, weren't you?"

He's clearly entranced by the idea. He *wants* me to have been murdered. I slide my legs underneath me — my right side hurts so much in this position — so I'm sitting with my knees bent. I shuffle my weight slightly so that I can be ready to take off. How fast will he be?

Very fast. He ran track in school. I saw it in his mind earlier.

"I know other things." My voice falters. I can't be murdered twice — can I? If all else fails I can just leave Ashley's body — right? But — what will happen if I can't?

He raises his eyebrows.

"Like, uh — things like —"

He doesn't seem to care that I know about the party. I thought it was important, I thought it would work. Dammit — what else do I know?

I've been watching Matt for the past eight months. I know a lot of things about him that Ashley wouldn't — things only a ghost, or perhaps a detective, would know.

"I know you come in late every morning that you're supposed to open the store. You talk Stacia and Vicki into covering for you when you want to leave early — which is pretty often because you're lazy. You like horror movies, you always get pepperoni and pineapple on your pizza, and you never drink tap water."

His face is completely blank.

"One night no one else was in the store and you danced around singing the songs from *The Sound of Music*."

His eyes narrow — is he starting to believe me? I glance at the doorway to my left, then back at him. Am I ready? Is it time? I hope against all logic that Savannah has freed her wrists, but I'm afraid to look at her because I don't want him to see if she has.

"You left a note for Savannah on the bulletin board. " His mouth starts to open. He must believe me by now. The words spill out, faster and faster.

"I know you want to 'be a murderer', that you want to kill both of these girls tonight. And I know that you tried to kill the girl at your fraternity house, but were too drunk to do it right. You screwed it up by drinking, just like your father always said you'd screw things up."

Matt lunges at me, arms outstretched, and I leap up and dash for the doorway in the east wall. He catches up to me before I'm anywhere near it. He's so much faster than I thought!

He grabs me around the waist, then pins my arms with his own and carries me back to my place in front of the backdrop, lifting me as easily as if I were a coat, or maybe a light tree branch. I squirm, but his grip is firm. He sets me on my feet, then smacks my left cheek so hard that I fall over.

As I fall my right hand flies out into my invisible wall, and I'm ejected from Ashley's body. The sudden lack of pain is startling, and I forget to catch myself as I fall hard on the floor.

I scramble to my feet. Matt pulls Ashley's body into a sitting position and props her up against the wall. Savannah's eyes are wide, and her cheeks glisten with tears.

"What the hell were you trying to do?" the spirit Ashley wails from somewhere behind me.

I shake my head, my eyes fixed on Matt.

"I was trying to distract him so Savannah could get the key. But it didn't work." It didn't work at all. Should I try again? He was so fast!

"A ghost, eh?" Matt mutters. He rummages in one of his bags and pulls out something small. A flash of light reflects off of it, but I can't tell what it is. Savannah follows his every movement.

Matt squats by Ashley's body and holds the shiny thing under her nose. It looks like a little glass vial. I push myself to my feet. Should I go back into Ashley's body? If I do, then what?

"Hey! What's he —" Ashley cries from behind me, then her voice stops. I turn around just in time to see her vanish. Oh no! I whip back around.

Ashley's body twitches several times, then she opens her eyes and blinks. Her mottled skin is so pale. Matt grins. "I brought smelling salts to make sure you were awake for the finale."

Ashley's eyes wander around the room as if she doesn't know where she is.

"Are you the ghost?" Matt asks her.

"Huh?" she replies. Her voice is soft and faint. She looks as though she might fall over at any second.

He snorts. "It's high time things got moving." He leans down, lifts up the left leg of his jeans, and pulls a nasty-looking knife out of a leather sheath that's strapped around his calf. He thrusts it forward, stopping when the point of the blade just reaches Ashley's throat. She blinks rapidly, her eyes trying to focus on the knife. Matt smiles. He looks happier than I've ever seen him. My heart pounds madly away inside my ghostly chest, but it's a faint pounding compared to what I felt in Ashley's body. The prickling in the back of my head and neck has grown to a buzzing. It's like having a beehive in my head. I rub my ears, but it won't stop.

"I have a surprise for you," he announced, his tone mocking. He thrust his fist out toward me, then turned it palm up and spread his fingers, revealing a shiny silver locket. A small heart on a thin silver chain, with a little "L" engraved on the heart. Lizzie and I each had a necklace just like the one he was holding — mine with an "E", of course. Uncle Jim had given them to us years before. Lizzie

never, ever took hers off, not even when we snuck out to jump in the pond in the brutal Colorado summer heat.

Ashley closes her eyes. Savannah is watching Matt's face. Her face is ashen, and her lower lip trembles.

"Your sister's awfully pretty." He grinned. The gaps in his teeth made him look even more monstrous than I already knew him to be. "I've got her upstairs — I thought it best that the two sisters be reunited."

"No!" I screamed. My voice was hoarse and raspy. Could she hear me? Could she escape?

"Run, Lizzie!" I heard a small sound from upstairs. Oh God, not Lizzie!

Matt grabs Ashley's shoulder, then brushes the edge of the blade against her neck. It barely grazes her skin, but I can see little beads of blood form when he pulls it back. A tear runs down her cheek.

"Why don't I bring her down?" He chuckles. "I don't want to keep you two apart. It just wouldn't be right." He dropped the locket on the floor and headed back up the stairs.

"No!" I yelled. I thumped across the floor, moving as fast as I could on my knees and elbows. This time I wasn't concerned about being quiet. I couldn't let him hurt Lizzie, little Lizzie, my baby sister! I scrambled up the steps as best I could with my arms and legs tied. I didn't even feel the pain in my wrist or my ribs — all I could think about was helping her, saving her.

He reached the top of the steps and disappeared through the door, then came back and stood in the doorway with something in his hand. I kept struggling up the steps, then realized he was holding Lizzie's head by her dark, curly hair. She screamed when she saw me. He tossed her to one side, out of my sight, then stomped back down the stairs, his boots clomping loudly on the stones.

"She came looking for you," he sneered. "I caught her pokin' around outside. I think she needs to learn a lesson or two."

He moved closer, stopping just out of my feeble reach.

"But first I need to make some room for her down here."

He held a piece of rope in one hand and a knife in the other.

The sound is now a roaring in my ears. I can't see, I can't think! Lizzie! Not Lizzie!

I fall to my knees and cover my face with my hands, but I can't hide from myself. Not anymore.

He killed Lizzie.

He killed me, and then he killed her. My memories are true — now that I remember them. My little sister ... I'd forgotten — I'd allowed myself to forget — for all these years. For over a hundred years. It was my fault. She'd come here looking for me. I couldn't save her.

And now I can't save Ashley and Savannah.

Fifteen

My dead body burns, guilt coursing through me like raging flames.

Lizzie died — because of me. She came looking for me, and he caught her — and he killed her. I can't let the same thing happen to Ashley. I can't fail Ashley too.

I jerk my hands away from my face.

Matt is still holding the knife up to Ashley's neck. I can only see his back, but Savannah's eyes are glued to his face, her mouth hanging open. Ashley's eyes are closed tight.

I push myself to my feet, then step forward and leap into Ashley's body, and this time into her mind as well.

It's not like before when I was in her body. Her spirit is here, with me. Yet there's something that is different from all the other times when I've touched the minds of the living. I can sort of feel her thoughts, but it's not like I'm thinking them, the way it has always been when I've touched the minds of others. It's like we're two halves of the same person. Always before I've been a visitor, a voyeur, in a living person's body and mind. This time I feel like a guest, privy to some things but not others.

Matt pulls the knife back from Ashley's neck and holds it up to examine the drops of blood in the light. Her neck stings where he broke the skin. Matt tilts the blade first one way, then another, his lips curved in a joyful smile.

"Hi, Emma." Ashley's voice sounds exactly the same as it always does, even though it's now in my head. Although I guess I'm in her head. Can she sense me the way I do her?

"Ashley? Can you hear me?"

"Sort of. I guess this is what you meant about touching someone."

"Ashley, I have a plan." She's not going to like this, but there's nothing else to try.

"What?"

"We — you — run up the stairs, and while Matt is chasing us, Savannah will grab the key and escape. I told her it's on the floor by the bed."

Ashley turns her head to look at Savannah. It's strange to be in her body, where I was just a brief time ago, and not be moving it. Can I control it? It doesn't seem polite to try, so I squelch my curiosity. I see Savannah through Ashley's eyes; the one open, the other still half closed because of her swollen eyelid.

"Oh, I see now, from what you're, uh, remembering. Weird. So *that's* what you were trying to do before. But what about me?" Her voice sounds plaintive. "He'll catch me, and then …"

I don't need to be able to read her thoughts to know what she's thinking.

"Savannah will tell the police, and they'll find Matt. He won't kill you — he'll be too busy trying to get away." Once the police know who he is he won't be safe anywhere in the country. He'll have to run. But will he kill Ashley anyway? He'll be a marked man, so what will he have to lose?

"You aren't sure. I know you aren't sure."

I can't pretend to be confident and calm, not anymore.

"You're right. Worst case … Worst case he'll kill you, but maybe we can at least help Savannah escape. And —" I pause. Can I go through this again?

"And if he does kill you, I'll be here with you. I promise I won't leave." I feel queasy. Being murdered once was more than enough. But it's the only thing I can offer.

Ashley thinks for a moment. I can't tell what she's thinking, but I can sense what she's feeling.

"Thank you, Emma," she says. I can feel her sincerity, and her fear, just like she must be able to feel mine. "But your plan won't work — it will take too long for her to get the key and open the door with her hands tied behind her back. And she's going to have to hop because her legs are tied up, so she'll be super slow."

"She can do it," I say firmly. I know Ashley can sense how unsure I really am, but she says nothing. "We just have to make sure we keep him away from her as long as possible. We have to give her as much time as we can."

Matt holds the knife up to Ashley's neck again. "Say something! Distract him!"

"I know you believe I'm a ghost," she tells him. Her voice shakes. I can feel the tightness in her chest, the fear coursing through her body.

He sneers. "If you were a ghost, then why did you collapse like that?"

Ashley sighs. "I'm a ghost — this isn't my body. So it's kind of hard for me to stay in it when someone like *you* pushes it around." Her tone is haughty. *"Is that good, Emma?"*

"That's great! Now see if you can get him to go back to his camera, or better yet, toward the door — you just need a little space so you can get started running. And Ashley —" I pause. *"I'll help you if I can. Good luck."*

Matt opens his mouth, but before he can say anything Ashley has leapt up and is running toward the doorway. What is she doing? She wasn't supposed to run until he was further away. I lend her my strength, my living strength, making her much faster than she would have been by herself. It's an odd feeling, allowing my energy to be used by her, but not controlling her body. I — we — hear Matt yelp, followed by a clatter punctuated by a lot of swearing. Savannah must have tripped him. The reprieve doesn't last long, though. We hear him following us — following Ashley — but we've got a head start. We can do it.

"Faster! Go faster!" I urge Ashley on. We — she — sprints across the room, through the doorway into the empty hall. She reaches out and grabs the knob on the door to the stairwell, pulling it open so hard it bangs against the wood paneling. The pain in her right side makes it hard to breathe. I try to concentrate on it, willing myself to feel the pain for her so Ashley can focus on running. We dash through the door, then turn left and speed up the stairs in the dark, holding on to the railings to help guide us. We're moving so quickly. I hear Matt behind us — we're fast with my living energy added to Ashley's, but he's almost as fast. We scurry up the steps, my — our — feet pattering on the worn wood. Ashley pounds on the door — "There's no one there!" I tell her, but she tries anyway. No one comes to rescue us, to rescue her — the store is empty. Her hands smack into the door, and she grabs the door handle, trying to turn it — it's locked, of course. But —

Sandra Connelly had a terrible memory. She was always losing keys, so she'd hide extra keys around the house — under rocks, in planters. On top of doorframes.

"Ashley!" She realizes what I'm thinking as soon as I think it. She reaches up and runs her fingers frantically across the top of the door.

The cold, hard metal of the hidden key is as precious as gold. Ashley grabs it and jams it in the lock. Matt's feet thump loudly on the wooden stairs, the sound echoing in the small stairwell as he comes toward us. He's slowed down. It's too dark for him to see what's going on, and he knows he's got us cornered. He laughs just as Ashley turns the key, twisting the doorknob while pushing as hard as she can on the door.

The old hinges squeak loudly as the door opens.

"Hey!" he yells.

We run out into the store, the shelves of movies familiar, almost comforting in their normalcy, but it's a deceptive comfort — Matt's almost here!

"Run out the front door!" I yell inside my — our — mind. Ashley starts for the main entrance — to safety! — and then a harsh grip on her arm pulls us back.

Matt wrenches her toward him, his strong fingers clenched tight around her arm. The moonlight shining in through the windows casts eerie shadows across his face, making his features solemn and sinister. The person on the inside is finally visible on the outside.

"Ashley, let me take over — please!" I feel a softening, a release, as Ashley relinquishes control of her body to me. My energy, my living energy, fills my blood — her blood, our blood — like electricity. Matt's grip is fierce, but I'm stronger than him. For the moment. I jerk my arm away, pulling with all the strength I can muster. He can't maintain his grasp, and my arm flies free. I tear for the door — I have to reach it, I have to. It's locked from the outside, but it's just a wooden frame holding a long pane of glass.

I close my eyes and thrust my arms out in front of me, clenching my hands into fists and holding my forearms perpendicular to the ground, then crash into the door. The glass fragments into a million pieces with a loud shrieking sound, almost like ice shattering, as Ashley and I crash through it. Tiny pieces of glass fly about, cutting me, landing in our hair. The bells on the door jingle merrily. I open my eyes as I land heavily on one foot, staggering as I catch myself. The air on the other side of the door is icy cold, and the light breeze makes my cut skin sting. I remember my invisible wall right as I hit it.

"Go, Ashley! Run!" I yell as I stop, stymied by my barrier. Ashley continues on, alone, but Matt leaps through the remnants of the door and grabs her. He pulls her back into the store.

"No!" I scream, and jump forward, into Matt.

He's livid. His anger fills him— and now me — with heat as he drags her back toward the door to the basement.

"Fucking bitch. You're no ghost." He's holding her arm so tightly it must be squeezing off her blood flow.

She's not, but I am.

His heart is beating fast. He's angry, oh, so angry that she almost escaped, furious that he now has to make sure the broken glass doesn't lead anyone to think to look in the basement.

"What did you say?" he asks Ashley. He shakes her so hard her very brains must be rattling. I can feel her skin under his hand, the stickiness of the blood on her arm. He wants to make her bleed more, to pay her back for causing so much trouble.

She didn't say anything. I did. I'm the ghost. I'm inside your head, Matt.

He's still moving toward the basement door. Ashley is struggling feebly; she barely has strength enough to stand. He's going to take her downstairs, beat her until she's unconscious again, rip off her tattered clothes, and —

I know what you're thinking, but you're not going to do any of those things. I'm inside of your mind, inside of you. And I won't let you.

"Who's talking? Who the fuck is saying this?"

I concentrate on his feet. I was able to control Ashley's body. His, as repulsive as he is to me, isn't any different. It's just a body.

His feet slow and he stops.

See? I'm in charge now.

Fingers. Relax the fingers.

His grip on Ashley's arm weakens. Not enough, but enough for me to tell.

"I don't understand. Who are you? Are you —" he stops himself, but I can read his thoughts.

Yes. I'm really a ghost.

I think about pain, all the pain I felt in Ashley's body, all the pain I felt when my murderer beat me, cut me, strangled me, raped me. I will all that pain into Matt's mind. I make him feel it, just as if it had happened to him.

"Please, please don't," he whimpers. His hand slides down, off of Ashley's arm, and he drops to his knees. A shard of glass stabs into his shin. "Please stop, it hurts, please."

Ashley catches herself, then stumbles across the broken glass and out the front door. I watch as she heads out into the parking lot, then down the street. A car zooms past her, then another and another. Her steps are slow and faltering now that I'm not there to help her, and she wraps her arms around herself against the chill. The cold doesn't bother me, but I hope it's not too much for Ashley. But cold or not, she's running — and she's safe. It's late at night, but there are far too many people about for Matt to try to catch her. She waves feebly to one of the cars — it slows and stops, and someone inside leans out to say something to her.

Ashley is free. I close my eyes tight for a second.

I turn around to see Matt staring at Ashley through me. I was so focused on watching Ashley that I didn't notice when he moved out of me. His eyes are fierce little ovals in his handsome face, and his beautiful mouth has become a tight narrow line. He runs back down the stairs to the basement, his feet thumping loudly on the wooden steps. I sprint after him, my joy at Ashley's escape dampened by my worry for Savannah.

He dashes through the door to the right of the stairs, with me close on his heels, then speeds through the doorway to the room where he had been about to kill Ashley. He skids to a stop as if he has brakes on his feet. I smile when I realize why he's stopped.

Shreds of duct tape and the sliced plastic zip tie lie in front of the open door on the west wall. Matt's knife lies among them, the blade glinting brightly in the moonlight that flows in through the doorway.

Savannah is gone.

Matt stands there for a minute, his mouth hanging open, his eyes open so wide I wonder if his eyeballs might fall out. I watch him, breathless myself, but filled with a smug happiness. They got away! Ashley and Savannah are safe!

Matt mutters something under his breath, then grabs his camera, stuffs it into one of the black canvas bags, and sprints out the open door, scooping up the knife on the way. He starts up the van and guns the motor, the angry sound loud in the silence of the empty room. His tires squeal as he races out of the parking lot, and I hear him speed away, grinning as I imagine how frustrated he must be.

They're safe!

They're both safe!

~~~~~

The police show up very quickly. Matt can't have been gone more than ten minutes, maybe not even that long. I sit on the floor in the southeast corner of the room in the basement and watch them scurry about. It's almost like watching a movie. They are very thorough; taking fingerprints, scribbling notes about things, stomping up and down the stairs, picking up pieces of evidence while wearing plastic gloves. Finally the hubbub dwindles away and the last officer leaves the room, turning off the lights and shutting the door, leaving me by myself in the basement of the store. Alone, just like always.

I wander back upstairs and sit on the checkered couch; it's cheery pattern looks gloomy in the early morning darkness. I hope Ashley will be okay. At least she's safe. Unlike Lizzie.

I smack the couch with a fist, its firmness solid against my intangible blow. How could I have forgotten about Lizzie? How could I have let her get hurt? She came looking for me. She got caught looking for *me*. It was my fault she got caught — my fault she died. My shoulders sag and I curl up in a little heap and cry. Lizzie died because of me. If only I could have saved her like I helped save Ashley.

I choke back a sob and stand up, sniffling, then take a deep breath and wipe my tear-soaked hands on the denim of my modern jeans. The sun will be coming up soon. I remember how beautiful it was to see the rosy light of morning stretch across the eastern plains, how the grasses moved softly in the dawn breeze. I haven't been able to see the plains for years. I walk along the wall, trailing my fingers lightly against it, absently following my regular route around the room, the path I use when I walk the boundaries of the old house.

My fingers run through the shelves to drag along the drywall underneath. There's where the original door was.

Fifteen steps to the old wall. I count them as I walk. One. Two. Will Ashley come back? Three. Four. Will I ever see her again? Five. Six. Seven. What will happen to Matt? Eight. Will they catch him? If they do, there can't be any question of his guilt. I hope he goes to jail for the rest of his life! Nine. Ten. Back in my time he would have been shot, or maybe hanged — and either would serve him right. Eleven. Twelve. If Ashley comes back, will I be able to speak to her? Thirteen. If I touch her, if I enter her mind, will she be able to sense me, or will it be just like touching anyone else? Fourteen. Fifteen. Sixteen.

I freeze in mid-step, my right foot frozen just above the floor.

I must have miscounted. It's fifteen steps from the old cherry door.

I look to my left, then my right.

I'm past my barrier.

Prickles run across my shoulders and down my back. I'm not thinking clearly. After the past few days, how could I be? I must have lost track of the number of steps.

I set my foot down and take one slow, halting step forward, then another. My breath catches. I'm past where the wall of the original house ended, I'm past it for sure.

I run forward, sprinting toward the west wall, the forbidden, unreachable wall. I reach it and smack it with the palms of my hands, giggling, full of confused delight. My boundaries are gone, inexplicably gone.

I slip through the wall and out into the parking lot. Over there is the door that Matt brought both Ashley and Savannah through. To my right is the street. I trot over and look up and down its length. I can hear a car somewhere nearby, on a neighboring street, perhaps. I dash across the road, over to the florist's shop, and press my face up against the glass, staring at all the beautiful flowers that are waiting for the light of day to be purchased, to be taken away to brighten people's homes and lives. I'll be able to see them, now, once daylight comes. I'll be able to see all the things I've never been able to reach. I laugh. I really am free.

I turn and stand on the sidewalk in front of the shop, looking across the street to the video store, to the house I know so well. I can go anywhere. Anywhere at all.

But where will I go? I'm no longer bound to the old house, but I'm still a ghost. I'm still alone.

The cool autumn wind blows through me. I do know where to go, I realize suddenly. But it isn't a place. Not really. I now know what I need to do to leave. I smile, take a few steps, then do a cartwheel in front of the florist's shop. My legs stay straight up in the air, just like Ashley's.

Will Ashley be okay? She'll recover from her injuries, but will she be okay?

I can't leave until I know. I look down the street to the east, the direction she headed every time she left the store. I could search for her, but I don't have any idea where to find her, and the town has grown so large I don't even know where to start looking. Someone at the store will surely say something about her, then I'll know if she's okay. And — maybe Ashley will come back. I want her to. I need to know she's all right. I can't leave. Not yet.

The rosy light of the rising sun warms me as I turn cartwheel after perfect cartwheel down the empty sidewalk.

Sixteen

The employees — and customers — talk about nothing else for the next week. Ashley and Savannah are apparently doing well and — thank heavens! — Matt has been caught and is now in jail.

I can leave now. I'm no longer bound to this place, nor to this existence. Every day I feel the pull of wherever it is that I can go to now — that I *should* go to now. I'm just not ready to leave yet.

Now that I can, I explore the neighborhood. It's so wonderful to be outside. It snowed a bit last night, a light sprinkling of snow. I stood on the sidewalk a few blocks over looking up at the cloudy night sky and watched the snowflakes drift down on me, through me. It might snow again today. The sky is a light gray, and when I walked outside a little while ago everything had that quiet muffledness that comes right before a heavy snowfall.

Every day I hope the same thing — that Ashley will come in, that she'll tell me she's okay. That I'll *see* she's really okay.

Today the store is quiet and peaceful. I sit on the red couch and watch the leaves blow by on the sidewalk outside, my arm propped up and my chin resting in the palm of my hand. Bells jingle softly on the new front door as someone comes in.

"Emma?"

I jump at the sound of my name. It's Ashley!

She's standing about five feet from me, peering around, but of course she doesn't see me. She's a little pale, but her cheeks are a healthy pink color. Her bruises aren't completely gone, but they've faded so much that someone who hadn't seen her before might not even notice. Her swollen eye looks completely normal, and there is a small bulge underneath her jacket where she must have a bandage or something supporting her broken ribs. No cartwheels for her for a while, I suppose. But she'll be able to do plenty after she heals.

She walks across the room and stops at the basement door, glances around to see if anyone is paying attention to her, then tries the doorknob. It's locked. She heads up the steps to the second floor. I trot after her.

At the top of the stairs Ashley heads straight for the green room. She stops in the middle of the empty room. I stand next to her, invisible, and we gaze together out the west window at the mountains. There's quite a bit of snow on them already, especially high up. The sun is getting low, and should set soon. The days are short at this time of year.

"Emma, if you're there," she says quietly, then takes a deep breath. "Thank you. Thank you for helping me. Thank you for saving me. Thank you for everything."

"You're welcome," I reply, even though I know she can't hear me, not anymore.

"I'm fine. I really am. I don't want you to worry about me." Her voice is filled with conviction. "I promise. I will be okay. But I wanted to tell you so you didn't worry. Savannah is okay too. She moved in with her aunt, and she's a lot happier. I'm so glad — I had no idea what she was going through until we talked at the hospital."

"I hope you can hear me, Emma! Because —" She pauses and clasps her hands together. "Because I found some things out that you need to know."

What? What on earth is she talking about?

"After you died they found your sister at that man's house."

My heart feels as though it's being held by fingers of ice. Oh, oh Lizzie …

Ashley takes a deep breath. "They caught him, Emma. They caught him, and your sister didn't die! I'm sorry you died. I'm so sorry. But they caught him!" Her tone is fervent. "They caught him! Your sister Lizzie lived to be eighty–four years old. She married a man named Ned Jacobson, and they had seven kids."

Even if she could hear me speak, I'd be speechless.

Lizzie didn't die? She married Ned?

It occurs to me that I should be jealous, but instead I feel a buoyant happiness.

Lizzie didn't die!

Ashley clasps her hands together.

"I hope you can hear me, Emma. There's no way I can thank you enough. No way at all. But I thank you from the bottom of my heart."

We stand there for a few minutes, then Ashley turns to go. I reach out and touch her shoulder with my hand, willing with all my might that she can sense my thoughts — just for a second. That she can sense my gratitude — my joy that she survived, and my thanks that she took the trouble to find out what happened to me — and to Lizzie.

I'm concentrating so hard that I can't feel Ashley's mind, but when she steps away I see her smile. "Goodbye, Emma," she says softly, and walks out of the room.

Seven kids? I grin.

I glance out the window. The autumn sun is setting, warming the snow-covered mountain peaks with a soft orangish-red glow.

It's time.

I close my eyes, and then …

About the Author

Jamie Ferguson lives in Boulder, Colorado, where she spends her free time attempting to tire out her two herding dogs. *With Perfect Clarity* is her first novel.

www.ingramcontent.com/pod-product-compliance
Lightning Source LLC
Chambersburg PA
CBHW050738180626
46814CB00002B/817